JONAS' ALPHA

Creekside Township Rivals

Book 2

JT Fader

This book is a work of fiction. The characters, incidences, and dialogue are drawn from the author's imagination and are not to be construed as real. Any resemblance to actual events or persons, living or dead, is entirely coincidental.

Published by Steambath Press
A Creekside Township Rivals Romance

Paperback published December 2023
ISBN-13: 978-1-998008-41-4

Chapter One | Jonas

The chaos started as soon as I opened the front door of our home. After a long day of work at *Growlers*, my restaurant, I usually had to field a million questions when I walked in.

"Uncle Jonas!" little Maddox shrieked and flung himself into my open arms. My nephew had just turned 6. He'd shifted into non-wolf form very near his fifth birthday. Right on schedule. He wouldn't shift back into wolf form until he was at least sixteen. At that point, he would gain access to the telepathic link of the pack. Until then, his audible voice couldn't be quietened.

"What's up?" I asked him.

"Brianna shifted today!"

"I heard." My niece Brianna had turned 5 years old four days ago. We'd all been anxiously awaiting her shift to see what her precious non-wolf form face would look like.

A beautiful young creature approached me.

"Unca," Brianna said. It would take a while until her speech caught up with her ability to understand language. I stroked her face. Dark hair and dark eyes. She looked like Adam.

"You're home later than usual." Adam waddled up to me, 7 weeks pregnant with four furry pups of varying ages dancing around his feet. Since the birth of their first pup Maddox, Lucas and Adam had been busy filling the house. A new pup every spring—like clockwork.

This time they were expecting twins.

With the addition of twins, we would be a household of eleven.

"Did you bring meat, Uncle?" Maddox asked.

Adam sighed. "He's been asking all day. The pups have eaten everything in the fridge."

"Luckily, I have a side of beef in the truck."

Lucas wandered into the room looking exhausted. "I'll help you with that." We were averaging a side a week supplemented by the few times a month Lucas and I were able to go hunting.

He was usually too tired. Working full days and then coming home to help Adam with the pups was wearing him out. I'd never seen him happier, though. They loved the large family they were creating. They were both in their element— so in love. They wouldn't be able to keep it up much longer. Adam was approaching forty, the typical end of the breeding age for male Omegas.

I was creeping up to my mid-30s. There was little chance I'd join the new family tradition of overrunning the pack with pups. I'd resigned myself to being an uncle.

Lucas followed me out to the truck, and we hoisted the side of beef out of the truck bed and headed for an outbuilding we used for preparing meat.

Once inside, we got to work sawing the animal into pieces that would fit in the fridge. Lucas was quiet. This close to the birth of one of his pups, he always went through waves of anxiety. Adam had become a pro at giving birth, but the uncertainty did a number on Lucas. He'd never be able to attend the birth of one of his pups and not think about the death of his chosen mate.

"You all right?" I asked him.

"Only one week to go."

"And you're sure it's twins."

"The humans at the hospital assured me their scanner is accurate. And there was no mistaking them on the screen. Two little bodies. Two little heartbeats."

"I suppose it was bound to happen eventually seeing as Carina has had two sets."

"We're running out of space. Now that Brianna has shifted, she and Maddox can share a room with bunk beds. The other four pups, though. There will be one shifting every year. And then the twins ... I'm not sure where we're going to put them all."

I smirked at him. "Have you considered slowing down?"

"Birth control is useless when Adam is in heat. We've proven that a few times."

"Maybe don't mate when he's in heat."

Lucas cocked an eyebrow at me. Apparently, that wasn't an option.

"Have you thought of using condoms?" I asked.

Lucas screwed up his face. "Adam is my fated mate. I'm supposed to plant my seed in him."

"Then you need to stop complaining."

"I'm not complaining. I'm just trying to figure things out."

This conversation was a long time coming. I knew it was coming. And now here it was. My big brother was going to ask me to move out.

"I can build my own house," I offered. "Some of the wolves in Carina's house are ready to make a move. Her place is getting crowded too. Plus, we'll need more housing eventually. Yours and Carina's pups are going to grow up and need somewhere to live."

"You wouldn't mind?"

Lucas' expression was one of despair *and* hope. His eyes were sad, but his mouth was poised to smile. His mind was probably popping off with firecrackers of relief.

"No, I don't mind. I'll get some of the wolves organized. Maybe hire a contractor who worked on that housing development outside town."

"You could probably use one of their house plans. There are some nice 5-bedroom homes in that neighborhood."

I stacked a pile of ribs on a piece of butcher paper and wrapped them up. "I'll work it out. Put enough wolves on the job and we can build the house in a few months. The weather is warm enough now. I don't think it'll snow again until winter."

Lucas wandered over and patted me on the shoulder. "I appreciate this. I don't like kicking you out. We've always lived together but I don't know what else to do."

"I'll move into the cabin for now. Give me a couple of days then you can have my room."

"Thanks again, Jonas."

"No need to thank me. I'd do anything for you and your family."

We finished wrapping the meat, piled it into a carrying bucket, and went back to the house. Maddox leaped around excited as I filled the fridge. The meat wouldn't last long.

If Lucas was too tired again this weekend, I was going to team up with a few other wolves from the pack and find some deer to fill the freezer. The bought meat was costing a fortune.

The family electrical business was doing well, so Lucas had a steady stream of money coming in, but the amount of meat consumed in the house was extreme.

He had to be hurting.

I tried to eat at the restaurant so I wasn't using any of the weekly meat deliveries to the house. I paid Lucas for my portion regardless but tried not to eat it.

I headed to my room. I had a date tonight with a wolf from the West Creekside pack. We'd dated years back, but our family had been busy welcoming new pups, and we were still getting a system in place. I couldn't devote enough time to a relationship.

Now, Lucas and Adam had it handled.

We'd be heading to my restaurant for dinner. It was always a strange experience, bringing dates to my place of work, but *Growlers* was the only restaurant in town. The only place one could get a hunk of meat for a meal outside their home. I was providing a valuable service.

I ended up in the kitchen after changing. I needed a beer before I headed into town.

"You look nice," Adam said.

I turned to face him. "Thank you."

Sometimes when Adam gave me compliments like that, it took me right back to the first time I met him. When I'd tried to pick him up on his first night in Creekside. Thankfully, he'd been too tired for a rut, or things would have been awkward between us now that Adam was my brother's mate. His fated mate. He was still nice to look at; tall and muscular—gorgeous face.

And he handled their pups with skill. He was a natural Omega.

I was proud to call him brother.

"Date?" Adam inquired.

"Yeah, Steven again."

"That's twice now … not to mention years ago. No connection?"

I shook my head. "Not mate material."

"He seems nice enough."

"I was talking about me." I'd given up waiting for my fated mate or trying to find someone to call my chosen mate. I only dated so I could get my pent-up rutting desires out of my system.

Adam laid his hand on my shoulder. "Please don't think that way. I thought I'd never be happy again. That I'd never find a mate who would love me. And look. Lucas came along."

"You moved 7 hours from home." Maybe that was the answer. Head for the city and join a wolf pack there. Maybe find a mate I could call my own. "Maybe I should do that. Move."

Adam wrinkled his brow. "Your family would be devastated. We love you."

I rolled my shoulders and downed my beer. I had to leave soon, or I'd be late for my date. I wanted to get the obligatory meal out of the way so Steven and I could get down to why we were seeing each other. I had already booked a room in the only hotel in town.

Neither of us could bring the other home with them. Living with family meant less privacy. I hated traipsing a wolf into the house with me. And now that there were pups in the bedrooms around mine, we had to be extra quiet. And that just wasn't me.

My rutting partners loved how vocal I was.

"I'm not going anywhere," I said.

Adam sighed. "Good." He shifted his weight to one hip. He was big this time around. His usual nesting routines were being curtailed by his size. He often found himself breathless.

"Did Lucas talk to you?" Adam asked.

"About moving out? Yes."

"It was a difficult decision for him."

"I realize that. I don't mind doing it." I smirked at Adam. "Having pups around is cramping my style. How is a single wolf supposed to get any action."

"You get plenty of action."

Adam was right. I was never short of rutting partners. None of them wanted to make me anything more than that, though. I wasn't desirable enough to become someone's mate.

"That said … I need to go."

"We'll see you in the morning?"

"No, I'll be home late tonight. Steven doesn't like to stick around and cuddle."

Adam frowned. "I'm sorry, Jonas. You deserve better."

I tried my best to smile. "It is what it is."

Adam patted my arm. "We can debrief if I'm still up."

Chances are, he would be. Adam hadn't been sleeping well. Up for water, I often found him sitting in the living room with a cup of chamomile tea in the middle of the night; paper and colored pencils strewn across the little table Lucas had set up for him.

He loved to draw.

Adam taught art classes at the community center. He'd given up working full-time as an electrician because of the pups. Lucas had encouraged Adam to pursue something in a field he loved. Now Adam taught a class once a week. Sometimes drawing. Sometimes painting.

He was talented at anything art related.

"Thanks, Adam." I nodded and smiled at him, then left, and jumped into my truck to head back into town. I'd barely been gone an hour. We were meeting at 7. Plenty of time to eat and rut at least once before midnight. Maybe a second time if I was lucky.

I loved being rocked—rutted into a mattress. It helped me forget how unhappy I was.

I pulled up outside the restaurant.

Through the window, I could see Steven sitting at the counter. Another meaningless date. My life was empty and pathetic. I hauled myself out of my truck.

I pasted on an exuberant smile as I walked in through the door and Steven turned to face me. He mirrored my fake excitement to be meeting up for dinner to talk when we both knew why we were there. Not sure who we were doing the precursor dance for.

After hugging each other, we slipped into the booth at the back of the restaurant. If I was being honest, I was hungry today. I usually only ate every three days or so. I had a slim figure I liked to retain. Other wolves were larger and taller than me. They often referred to me as being petite.

Embarrassingly, I wasn't even bigger than most human males. I straightened the light, black turtleneck sweater I was wearing and signaled the human server to bring us ribs.

"How have you been? I asked. The obligatory small talk.

"Busy." Steven was a housing contractor. I'd decided I would be hitting him up to take on the job of building my new house sometime during the evening. "How's the restaurant business?"

"Barely afloat to be honest. As usual. Not many people in town want to eat out. We're only really busy for brunch and lunchtime."

Steven looked around. "Yeah, the place is pretty dead."

Change the subject.

"Are you having success on your recent hunts?"

"Plenty," Steven replied. "When was the last time you were out?"

"It's been weeks."

Steven looked at his hands. "We could hunt together."

I wrinkled my brow. That was the first time Steven had ever asked me to do something other than meet and rut. I felt the need to curtail any evolvement of the relationship.

"That would be crossing a line, Steven."

He looked up at me. "I know. I had hoped you might feel the same way as me."

That wasn't true. His greeting upon my arrival had been forced. If he had feelings for me, he sure knew how to hide them. There was only one reason for the suggestion.

"Are you being pressured to make me your mate?"

Steven sighed and nodded his head. "Our leader, Carl, says what I'm doing with you is wrong."

"So old fashioned. Next, he'll be saying as an Omega, I should have a chaperone on dates."

"He suggested that might slow you down."

I leaned back and crossed my arms. "So basically, your pack leader called me a slut."

Steven's gaze locked on mine. "You do have a reputation." There was heat burning in his eyes. The thought of me submitting to all those other wolves made him hot. And he loved telling me how dirty and nasty I was for rutting with humans as he was drilling me hard with his cock.

Steven was fun in bed.

The ribs arrived at the table. We made quick work of them. We barely made it through the door of the room I'd secured for the night before we were all over each other.

Truth was, our relationship bordered on hatred, but that worked for us. Steven liked to degrade me in bed, and I loved being on the receiving end of it.

It's how I felt about myself.

Chapter Two | Damon

Creekside was smaller than I remembered it being. When I contacted the town council president, he assured me there would be sufficient patronage for my business.

Now I wasn't so sure.

I pulled up outside the building I had bought sight unseen. I had studied the pictures the realtor sent me but hadn't felt it was necessary to make the 7-hour trek to check it out.

It was a no-brainer. Competition was too stiff in the city. I'd been floundering; barely staying afloat. I could have tried a different profession, but cooking and food sales were my passion.

Two years ago, I had driven through Creekside, and it had called to me. There was something about the quaintness of the place that stirred a desire in me for a quiet life. The little shops and houses lining the streets. The smell of woodsmoke in the air. All of it whispered peaceful.

It's what I needed. I was burnt out from city life. I'd lived my entire life in the inner city. It was harsh and dirty. I hadn't been able to get that drive through Creekside out of my mind.

One thing the town council president had warned me about, though. There were a large number of wolves living in Creekside. A concentration you didn't see in the city. Wolves tended to avoid city centers. Too noisy and fewer opportunities to hunt.

I'd been told that they weren't a problem. I was counting on them being civilized and frequenting town. My restaurant was designed partially around them. It had been a dream of mine to operate a meat market, delicatessen, and restaurant in one space. I opened my first one in the city three years ago. I gained exuberant regulars but not enough of them to pay the bills.

I had to move somewhere less expensive.

I unloaded the luggage out of my truck and grabbed a couple of the rifles I had brought with me. I wouldn't be selling strictly beef, pork, chicken, and bison. The plan was to head into the massive forest surrounding the town and hunt for wild game to sell in my store. That's where the wolf clientele figured into my plans. Surely, there were times they didn't feel like hunting.

I was counting on it.

According to the town council president, I needed to introduce myself to the two pack leaders in town before I started hunting. If I didn't, they would interpret my actions as hostile.

I did not need that. I had only ever spoken to a wolf once in my life. And that had been in elementary school. Kindergarten to be exact. The wolf had just sat there—non-verbal. The teacher had explained to us that the wolf's vocal cords weren't developed enough yet to speak.

It had struck me as odd. When he finally did speak, his voice was low and commanding. Sometimes he would growl if he didn't get his way. He made me nervous. I was glad when his pack decided to move on and set up in the countryside somewhere.

Since then, I hadn't knowingly spoken to a wolf. I'd seen a couple on the streets. They had been easy to spot; towering head and shoulders above the humans around them.

I knew very little about them. I had done a search on the Internet before moving here. They were separated into a hierarchy. Alphas, Betas, and Omegas. The Alphas were at the top. Their leaders were Alphas only sharing the top spot when they found a mate. The Betas oversaw the finer details of the pack. Making sure the rules were being maintained. They were also information gatherers; keeping the pack leader informed of any changes or concerns regarding the members.

Then there were the Omegas. They were the bottom of the pack unless they were mated to a leader. They were the ones—females and males, who were expected to produce offspring.

Male pregnancy confused me, and I'd had to look up a diagram to see how it was possible. Sure enough, male Omegas had a uterus just past their prostate. Ovaries—the whole bit.

It made me shiver a little with repulsion. I would have to get used to it. I'd been told the wolf population was growing exponentially of late. Something about a baby boom.

Some of those pregnant Omegas were bound to be male.

I unlocked the door of my new business. I was lucky, the building came with an apartment upstairs. It was already furnished, so that was a bonus. The only things of my own I'd brought in the form of home furnishings were some sheets, towels, and a few pictures.

I walked through what would be my store. I would investigate more later. I opened the door to the apartment and mounted the long flight of wooden stairs. The top of the stairs opened straight into the middle of the kitchen. I suppose that would be easier for groceries.

The kitchen had yellow walls and an orange backsplash. Someone had thought it would brighten up the place. The cabinets had been painted white with a brush. The brushstrokes were obvious. I touched the counter. Chipping Formica, likely from the 70s. The same with the kitchen table. The wooden chairs looked serviceable. Again—painted white.

At least it was clean.

It would have to do. I wandered into the living room through a doorway off the kitchen. I groaned. The 70s theme continued to the furniture in this room. I wish I had asked for pictures of the apartment before I purchased the building. I might have asked them to burn the contents.

I leaned my rifles against the side of the sofa. I would need to buy a new safe for them. I hadn't wanted to bring my old one. It was too heavy, and the combination dial was getting finicky.

I opened a doorway. Bathroom. It was sufficient. Somewhat updated. Clean.

I held my breath as I opened the door to what I knew would be the bedroom. I exhaled and threw my suitcase onto the bed. It wasn't too bad.

A queen-sized bed that would suit me fine. I needed my space in bed to stretch out. I was tall. Almost 6'4. But I wasn't a big guy. I kept my body in shape but had never bulked up.

There was a long wooden dresser down one wall. Two bedside tables and a comfy-looking recliner. A closet at the far end. It was a large room considering the size of the apartment.

The drawers were lined with pink flowered Mactac. It soon disappeared beneath my t-shirts. I'd only packed some of my clothing. The rest would be arriving in a small shipping container that would be delivered tomorrow. Also inside was the glass-fronted display case that would hold my meat and delicatessen items. I'd pulled it from my old business. The new tenants didn't need it.

The rest of the container was filled with dry goods like bags of pasta, jars of mustards and relishes, and a sizeable collection of BBQ sauces. And the many boxes with the rest of my clothes.

Not that I'm a clothes horse, but I like nice things. My collection of watches was my pride and joy. The suits came next. Then the shoes—definitely the shoes.

I opened the closet. It was going to be a tight fit getting everything in there. I might have to buy a freestanding wardrobe to go in the room.

By the time I finished unpacking, my stomach was grumbling.

I lifted an insulated bag from my luggage and went to the kitchen. I had packed two pastrami and lettuce sandwiches for my trip. I'd eaten one earlier. The one left would do for dinner.

I sat at the table and looked around as I ate. I owned this. I'd never owned a piece of property in my life. Now my home and business were mine. Or the banks to be more accurate. I'd had to take out a hefty mortgage to afford what I needed. Even in Creekside, the buildings weren't cheap.

In the city, though, I would never have been able to afford to buy my own building for my store. Owning this place gave me the sense of permanence I'd been craving.

I looked at my watch. It was late. Coming up on 10 pm. I made my bed. Along with the solitary pillow I'd stuffed into my luggage, the whole ensemble looked inviting.

I didn't have to argue with myself to go to bed earlier than usual. I was beat. The shipping container would be coming tomorrow morning. I needed to be up and ready early. I'd haul everything out of it on my own that I could, then I'd need to put up an advert somewhere looking for a couple of strong guys to help me with the rest. Maybe I'd meet my first wolves.

It was deathly quiet as I closed my eyes. For a moment I thought I wouldn't be able to sleep without the sounds of the city filling my room with chatter, honking, and sirens.

I was wrong.

I passed out cold.

THE NEXT MORNING WAS SUNNY. A perfect spring day. The kind of day you wanted when you were moving. The truck with the shipping container arrived on time and I received a few concerned looks from residents walking by on the far side of the street.

I was the new guy, and I was cluttering up the road.

It was temporary. The truck would be back in 3 days to pick up the empty container. I just needed to find someone to help me unload the heavier items.

I looked at the small map I had downloaded and printed. There was a community center halfway down the street. It was the most likely place for a bulletin board.

It was a pleasant walk down the street. I was able to nod to a few people and bid them, "Good morning." Everyone I passed seemed friendly.

I pulled open the doors of the community center. Sure enough, just inside, there was a corkboard covered in notices and business cards.

I perused a few and decided it would be a good place to post notices when I was looking for employees. Front and center, a full sheet advertising drawing classes happening right there at the community center. It was an old notice. The classes had started already.

They were happening right now.

I stuck my notice on the board. Curious, I walked into an open room through a second set of doors. Inside were people sitting at tables arranged in a circle, drawing. A typical bowl of fruit sitting on a table in the middle. Walking around peering at the student's work, a tall muscular man. His back was to me. The doors swung closed and banged behind me.

He turned around and I nearly fell over.

He was pregnant—his belly was quite round. I must have been staring.

He placed his hand on the protrusion. "Twins."

His voice was low and rumbling and I could now see how broad his chest was. I'd read Omegas were smaller than Alphas. Seeing his size was putting me off talking to the pack leaders.

Exactly how big was this guy's Alpha?

How big would a pack leader Alpha be?

He was watching me with curiosity. I realized I hadn't answered him.

Speak.

"I'm sorry. I'm new in town. I was checking out the community center."

"Well, welcome. A few years ago, I was new here too. It's an adjustment." His lumbering form approached me, and he reached out his hand. "I'm Adam Black."

"Damon … Lister." My hand was almost swallowed in his grip, but his shake was gentle. With his other hand, he rubbed his belly.

"How far along?" I asked.

"Almost 8 weeks."

My eyebrows shot up. "Aren't you a little big for only 8 weeks?"

"Pups grow faster than human babies. I'm due to have them any time now."

"Do you have others?" Not sure why I was getting so personal. But I found Adam fascinating. A big muscular guy talking about being pregnant like it was no big deal.

And there was a softness about him. His voice was low, but it was soothing. With his handshake, he'd been careful not to hurt me.

"We have 6 at home. 2 shifted—4 not."

"Shifted?" I knew what I thought it meant but I needed clarification.

"Yes, 2 of our pups are in non-wolf form. 4 are still furry bundles of joy."

I had more questions, but it didn't seem polite to ask them. Next best thing.

"That's a handful."

"My mate and I are kept running, that's for sure."

I perused the people still busy drawing. They all appeared to be human based on the size of Adam. I held out my hand to him. "It was nice meeting you, Adam. I'll let you get back."

Again—a gentle handshake.

"You as well. Maybe my mate and I will see you around."

"That would be fantastic." I waved at him as I backed up, then turned and headed outside. The sun was still shining but clouds were gathering. I needed to unload some of the container before it started raining. As well as my clothes, I had a few smaller kitchen items for the store. Mainly a meat slicer, a mixer, and a scale. The rest could wait until I had some help.

I smiled as I walked through my store.

I'd just met and conversed with my first wolf.

He had been more civilized than I'd been expecting. Gracious, welcoming, and teaching an art class at the local community center. Sure, there was the pregnancy that still didn't sit well with me, but he seemed as nurturing toward his unborn baby as any pregnant woman I'd ever met.

Maybe his mate wouldn't be too bad.

No sooner had I unloaded my portion from the container than two men showed up. They'd seen my advert. It took a bit of manhandling, but we soon had the display case inside the store.

I paid them in cash, and they went on their way.

I wandered into a room where the kitchen would be located. This is where the bulk of my money was going to go. I had a commercial kitchen company coming in a few days to take measurements and draw me up a plan. It would take another 3 weeks for it to be installed.

Meanwhile, I'd need to get plumbers and electricians in here to prepare the two rooms. There was one plumber in the next town over and an electrician right here in town.

I furrowed my brow.

Black's Electric.

Adam's last name was Black.

It seemed I might be meeting an Alpha wolf very soon.

Chapter Three | Jonas

I leaned on the counter as I looked across the street at the massive shipping container blocking my sight line of the building across the street from my restaurant. I'd asked around the packs and no one knew who was moving in or what they were planning on doing with the building.

I might have to talk to the humans.

Or I could just head over there and find out for myself.

I decided on the latter. My manager was buzzing around behind me. She could hold down the fort while I went across the street. The restaurant was only half full.

"Can you watch the shop?" I asked her.

"Where are you going?"

"To see what the heck is happening across the street."

"As long as you report back."

"Of course." I waved my hand at her, indicating she would hear the whole scoop. I left the restaurant, my curiosity ramping up as I crossed the street. It was almost warm as I walked across the sunny street. Warm enough to go out without a coat.

Especially with my inner wolf furnace burning.

I wandered around the end of the container and peered in the window. All I could see was an empty room and a glass-fronted display cabinet. The kind you see at a butcher's shop. Whoever it was would find most people went to the small grocery store in the middle of town for meat.

Maybe they had something else planned.

"Can I help you?"

I leaped back. I hadn't heard the door open I'd been so focused on snooping. Nice shoes. I sniffed the air. Human. "Sorry … just looking." I raised my gaze to the human's face.

Oh … my.

He was beautiful. Dark unruly hair landed in swoops all over his head and his eyes were dark, reflecting the sunlight like pools of water. And his jawline was absolutely lickable.

"You're not the first," he said.

"We don't often have anything new happen around here." I smiled at him. God, he was sexy and gorgeous. "I hope you'll excuse us for being curious."

"So far, everyone has been very hospitable."

"Oh … good. Creekside is a friendly place." Especially, in my jeans at the moment. My cock was very interested to find out more about this newcomer. Was there a Mrs. or Mr. Sexy?

"How long have you lived here?" he asked.

"All my life. My family has been living here for four generations."

The guy who would be haunting my erotic dreams leaned against the doorframe of his building, relaxed as could be. "Wow. You don't have any desire to go anywhere else?"

"No, I'm content here."

"What do you do for a living?"

I hitched my thumb over my shoulder. "I own the restaurant across the street."

His eyes opened wide. "Oh."

I furrowed my brow. "Oh? Why oh?"

The guy walked a few steps toward me allowing me to study him. He was tall but lean. Probably gloriously muscled. He moved closer. I was as tall as the bottom of his chin. My stature sometimes irritated me. Not sure why I ended up so much smaller than other wolves.

"I promise, I was assured there weren't any restaurants in town," he said.

I clenched my teeth. Damn humans. They had lied about the existence of my business. I knew for a fact the president of the town council had it in for me.

"It's not the main thing about my business," he continued. "But as well as selling meat and deli items, I will have some tables for people to order food."

I almost growled. My canines certainly ached in their sockets. I had a set of personal rules I lived by, though. One of them was I didn't wolf out on humans.

But I was pissed.

"I'm sorry ... what?"

"It'll be kind of like a bistro."

"That serves food." My hands rolled into fists. "A bistro is just another name for a restaurant."

"I'm only going to sell some soups, salads, sandwiches ... and desserts."

I almost surged at him. I had to call up all sorts of restraints to stop my legs from sending my body rocketing toward him. "So, exactly what my best sellers are."

"Mine will attract a different clientele." His gaze heated as it bore into me. I wasn't sure if I was about to be hit with condescension or if he was going to haul me inside his store and fuck me.

"With the deli there, they'll be expecting more of an upscale experience," he added.

Okay. Condescension it is.

I pressed my finger to his chest.

"So, you're calling my place cheap and pedestrian?"

"No. I just don't think there will be much crossover."

"Now you're calling my customers common."

"Maybe some people in town are looking for something different."

"I think you'll find you're wrong about that. People have been coming to my restaurant for two of those four generations. They're not going to stop now to visit some boutique joint."

"Your place is pretty wide open. Do you serve the town's entire population?"

What?

I crossed my arms and gripped my chest. "Are you talking about the wolves?"

"Yeah, you don't have much privacy for them to eat in peace."

"I have a back booth they feed in just fine." I nearly snorted out a laugh. This human had absolutely no idea I was a wolf. And I wasn't about to let on that I was.

"Maybe you should do some research about wolves," Damon said. "What I'm going to be offering will satisfy the wolves of this town as well as the humans."

If I continued this conversation any longer, I was going to burst out laughing and ruin my plans to keep my wild identity from this sexy but oblivious human.

"I'm going to go," I said. "Have fun with your little business." Before he could say a word in response, I stalked back across the road. The bells on the front door clattered, I opened it so hard.

I headed straight for my office and dropped into my chair.

Me: *"Lucas!"*

Lucas: *"What?"*

Me: *"Across the street. Some human is opening a restaurant."*

Lucas: *"I hadn't heard."*

Me: *"No one did. The town council didn't mention anything to you?"*

Lucas: *"Why would they? He's not a wolf."*

Me: *"He's in direct competition with me. Right across the damned street. I went over there to see what was happening with the building. He was an absolute bitch to me."*

Lucas: *"What do you want me to do?"*

Me: *"Make him leave. Scare him off. Make him disappear."*

Lucas: *"I can't do any of those things. He's a human."*

I slammed my hand down on my desk. If the potential customer stealer was a wolf, he would've had to report to Lucas and Carl. Ask permission to set up his business.

His request would have been denied.

Lucas: *"Is his name Damon?"*

Me: *"I don't know. I didn't ask. It wasn't exactly a friendly conversation."*

Lucas: *"Someone named Damon left a message on my answering machine. He wants a quote on wiring up his business for a kitchen. I had hoped he was calling from Riverton."*

Me: *"You're not going to do the work, are you?"*

Lucas: *"Of course not. He'll have to bring in someone from further out."*

Me: *"Thank you. I knew you'd have my back."*

Lucas: *"You're my brother. I wish I could do more."*

Me: *"Promise me you won't shop there."*

Lucas: *"Shop?"*

Me: *"Yeah, he's going to have a butcher counter and a deli as well. Says he's going to cater to the wolves better than I've been doing."*

Lucas: *"What do you think that means?"*

Me: *"I think you'll be getting a visit about hunting our territory."*

Lucas: *"That'll be a* hell no."

Me: *"And what about West Creekside?"*

Lucas: *"I'll talk to Carl. He won't want a wolf-owned business threatened."*

I felt better. This Damon wouldn't be able to bring any local wild game into his shop. His other items could be bought at the grocery store. And people in town would be loyal to me.

I sighed.

Or would they be? Most of my customers were human. Having a human-owned restaurant might draw them away from me. Especially if we had similar menus. They wouldn't care if they had to spend more at Damon's store. I was an Omega wolf. The humans had never respected me.

The only thing that would save me would be the size of my restaurant. Damon's building didn't have much floor space. It had been a clothing store last. The back room wasn't big enough for a full-service kitchen. And I knew the exact size of it. I'd been pressed up against every surface in that back room, one of the male wolf employees taking long breaks with me back there.

That relationship ended when he told me I had the temperament to become his chosen mate, but he was looking for someone equal in stature to bear his pups. He didn't want an Omega who might give birth to runts *like me*. It was at that point, something shut down inside me. I never viewed another wolf I was rutting with as a potential mate ever again.

I reached for a tissue. I hadn't meant to bring myself to tears. Most of the time, I was hardened against any soft-hearted emotions. Damon had upset me—made me doubt my life.

He didn't have the right to do that.

But I had no recourse. He was there. I was here. I would do my best to retain my customers. He would do his best to steal them. We would be at odds until one of us broke.

And it sure as hell wouldn't be me.

I flicked on my computer. I had the advantage of being established. I had no rent or mortgage payments to make. My costs were food, employees, and standard operating costs.

Unless he paid cash for the building across the road and was independently wealthy, I could undercut him into the ground. I went to work creating a series of marketing plans.

DURING THE THREE WEEKS, there was quite a bit of activity across the road. Plumbers, electricians, kitchen installers, and construction crews. All from out of town.

The wolves of Creekside Township had the trades sewn up. Lucas had kept his word. Not a single local wolf-owned business would go near Damon and his store.

It looked as though the wolf pack in Riverton had denied him service as well. The trucks parked across the street had phone numbers from much further away.

Good.

It was probably costing him extra.

There was still a construction crew working when Damon pulled away in his truck. I hauled off my apron, tossed it on the counter, and sprinted across the road.

I needed to see.

The wood floors were covered in cardboard. They'd probably been refinished. Behind the butcher case a long cabinet with shelving. One shelf up high. Beneath that, a blackboard to display the meat prices and specials. Near the window was a spread of shelving. In front of those, boxes, probably full of products he'd be selling as part of his delicatessen. Some of the shelves had wicker baskets on them. I turned to wander the restaurant portion of the store. There were six small round tables, stacked tabletop to tabletop. And an assortment of cute wrought-iron bistro chairs.

I came to a stop. At the back of the space were booths. Three of them. They had opaque sliding doors like the kind you see in Japanese restaurants. I opened one. The table and seating in the interior were designed to accommodate diners of a more generous size.

Wolves.

I'm going to kill him.

I caught his scent before he even entered the building. It was a combination of musk, soap, and woodsmoke. The combination reminded me of the cigars my sire used to smoke.

"Damon."

I turned to face him. He looked flustered.

"Not now," he said to me. "I have problems to deal with."

He raced around behind the butcher case, picked up a phone book, and began scanning it.

"Anything I can help you with?"

"Not unless you have an in with the Riverton pack." He ran his hand through his hair, setting it askew, then slammed his hand on the metal top of the case.

I smirked. Damon was adorable when he was aggravated. The poor human was getting pushback from the wolf packs in Creekside for wild game. He wanted to turn to Riverton.

Me: *"Hey, Lucas. Did you deny Damon hunting rights?"*

Lucas: *"Yesterday. Carl did today."*

I smiled. He would have to drive an hour west to Riverton and then trek into the woods there to do any hunting. It would be an entire day lost at least once a week.

It wouldn't stop him, but it would slow him down.

"Are you looking for hunting rights?"

"I had hoped I would be able to hunt locally ... but apparently not."

"They'll charge you money ... the Riverton pack," I said.

Damon looked up at me. "Are you serious? They don't own the forest."

I tipped my head and laughed. "Yeah, they kind of do. If *you* did your wolf research, you would find that wolves have ownership over the lands their territories are on."

"Then I'll hunt outside those areas."

"And you'll know when you're about to cross into their territory ... how?"

"Maps."

I had to scoff at that. "Humans don't have access to wolf territory maps."

Damon turned a lovely shade of crimson. His distress had the Omega in me wanting to make him feel better. Make him a nice cup of tea or suck his cock until he forgot why he was upset.

"Then what do I do?"

Not sure why I did it, but I answered honestly. "Pay the Riverton wolf pack for hunting rights. But be careful. Check with the leader before each hunt. Make sure he hasn't changed his mind."

I continued.

"The leader's name is Mark Simpson. He'll be in the book."

Damon sighed and scrubbed a hand through his already fucked up hair.

"I'm in over my head," he said.

"You haven't dealt with wolves before."

"Never." He came out from behind the butcher case. "You know what I think? I think the wolves own all the trade companies in this town. And for some reason, they turned against me."

"You're human." It was only a portion of the answer to his unasked question. I was enjoying having Damon think I was on his side—species-wise.

"So, you've had similar problems?"

I shook my head. "My family has been here forever. They don't play those games with me."

"You're lucky."

I pointed over my shoulder at the booths. "Not sure those will be used as intended."

"You don't think the wolves will eat here?"

"I told you. My restaurant has been feeding them for generations."

"But I'll have wild game."

"They can get that themselves for free. Why would they *pay* you for it?"

"Maybe they're busy. Don't have time to hunt. Or don't feel like it."

I laughed. "Wolves *always* feel like hunting. It's the everyday stuff that drives them crazy."

Damon studied me and his features softened. There was such depth behind his eyes. And his dark lashes were amazing. I could imagine them fluttering in ecstasy as he filled me with seed.

"You know a lot about wolves," he said.

"Been around them my entire life. Even went to school with a few."

"I met one a few weeks ago. Adam Black?"

"Oh, yeah … I know Adam."

"He was *really* pregnant."

"*Was*. Adam had his twin pups two weeks ago. Two furry whimpering bundles. Both Omega males. Their sire Lucas is ecstatic about them."

"You know them well."

"Their sire is the leader of the East Creekside pack. We all know Lucas and Adam."

Damon looked around, checking his surroundings. His voice was lowered when he spoke. He needn't have bothered. The construction crew had packed up and left.

"The whole male pregnancy thing doesn't bother you?"

"No." I wasn't sure what he was asking. "How else would they have pups?"

"With a female."

"But they're both males." I knew the humans did a thing called surrogacy where a female carried the offspring when a couple couldn't have any of their own or they were both male. Nature had never placed restrictions like that on us. Most types of mating pairs could have pups.

"I'm not used to it," Damon said. "Seeing Adam shook me up a little."

"If you saw him with them, though. He's so good with those pups."

"I sensed that." Damon focused on me. His eyes wandered up and down my body. In a different setting, I would have taken that as a sign and invaded his personal space.

"You know my name," Damon said. "You've never told me yours."

"No one has filled you in about me?"

"I haven't spoken to anyone local other than Adam. I've spent the past three weeks working with people from neighboring towns."

It was time.

I held out my hand. "I'm Jonas … Black."

Damon couldn't have scurried backward faster if I'd pushed him.

"Black?" His dark eyes were blown wide. "The same Blacks? Black's Electric?"

"Lucas is my brother."

The puzzle pieces finished falling into place. "You're a wolf?"

"Guilty."

"You don't look like a wolf."

"I've been told that."

Damon regained himself, his confidence returning, and pointed a finger at me. "You're why the wolves in this town won't work with me."

"I may have pulled a few strings."

"They won't shop and eat here, will they?"

"Not unless my brother says they can."

"And he won't."

"Nope." I wandered over to the butcher case and ran my finger along the glass. "Humans appreciate a good cut of venison too. Rabbits even. The grocery store doesn't carry those things."

"Oh … so now you're trying to help me."

"Just being neighborly."

"Well, I've had enough of this neighborly visit."

"Pity." I spun and headed for the door. I turned back and winked at him. "I was going to tell you about the research you recommended I do on wolves."

Okay, now he looked angry. I wasn't sure if I liked angry Damon.

I studied him.

Maybe I did. It made him *super* sexy.

Chapter Four | Damon

I clutched my head as Jonas bounded across the street. He looked far too giddy to be a wolf. My discomfort must have entertained him. He'd deliberately withheld his being a wolf from me.

Oh. My. God.

I watched him pull open the door of his restaurant. I leaned my forehead against the cool glass of my front window. He was the most beautiful and lithe creature I'd ever set eyes on.

Dark hair. Short on the sides and fun up top and gorgeous green eyes. Every part of his face was pure perfection. Especially his lips. It had been difficult to take my eyes off them.

His looks didn't match with the fact he was a wolf. In the human world, he would be considered a twink. The way he had sized me up revealed his affinity for men.

I backed away from the window. I'd never been this attracted to someone. A male someone. Never. Maybe it was his feminine nature. The way he had winked at me had nearly dropped me.

I needed to distract myself.

I turned to face my store. Maybe the booths would appeal to humans. A fun little privacy area they could book for intimate gatherings. Maybe I should think about getting a liquor license.

Yeah, definitely.

I headed for the phone, pulled out the number for the town council, and put a call in regarding a liquor license. I needed to go to the town hall and fill out an application.

Tomorrow.

Right now, I needed to sit down. Not only had Jonas been affecting my breathing, but my cock had responded to him. Thickening.

I was so confused. I'd never had my body respond to a man before.

Man.

He's not a man ... he's a wolf.

He looks like a man. A man I could imagine myself kissing. I groaned. Kissing and fucking until he cried my name. Instinctively, I knew his voice lifted in ecstasy would be so sweet.

My cock hardened.

Sitting down was no longer what I wanted. I ran to the stairs leading to the apartment. I jogged up them, my desire growing as I thought about Jonas.

My pants were open by the time I hit the kitchen. My underwear was damp with precum. I wrapped my hand around my cock. A few pumps and I spilled all over the kitchen floor.

I fell to my knees, my cock still in my hand.

So confused.

I imagined his lips on mine. So soft—so tender. Him sighing and moaning as we devoured each other. Tongues tangling. Tasting him. Traveling to the skin behind his ear.

My cock hardened in my hand.

I stroked it slowly. It didn't take much to encourage it. This time I imagined kneeling behind Jonas, thrusting my cock into him. Each stroke of my hand matched the movement of my hips.

I rocked my cock into my hand and closed my eyes.

I wonder if he'd howl.

I added that image and sound into my fantasy.

Jonas groaning and howling.

I grunted and came hard, adding to the cum already on the floor.

Twice.

He'd made me cum twice. No woman had ever done that to me. I struggled to my feet and collected some toilet paper to clean up my mess. I needed to buy paper towels.

A knock on my apartment door had me scrambling to do up my pants. Decent as I could manage, I headed down the stairs and opened the door.

It was Jonas.

"I forgot something," Jonas said and reached for my face. He pulled me down to him and caressed his lips onto mine. At first, I was too shocked to kiss him back, and then my body took over. I cupped his face and deepened the kiss. It was everything I had imagined and more. His taste was intoxicating. Any longer and I was sure I'd become addicted to it.

Jonas pulled away and licked his lips.

"Better," he said. "Now I can work without wondering."

"Wondering what?"

"Whether or not you're attracted to me."

"Now you know."

"That I do." Jonas turned from me and headed across the shop's floor. I wasn't sure if I should let him go. I wanted him in my bed. I followed him to the front door.

I kept the door pressed closed as he went to open it.

"You not letting me go?" Jonas said, facing me. His eyes studied mine. Then he blinked and I knew exactly what I wanted from him.

"I don't want to let you go."

"And what do you want?"

"You."

Jonas smirked at me. "What about the fact we're business rivals?"

"That kiss set rivalry aside."

Jonas ran his hand up my chest to my throat to the back of my neck. He pulled me down for another kiss. This one had me locking the door.

I lifted him and he wrapped his legs around my waist. He felt like he barely weighed anything. With our lips still busy, I walked to the apartment door and ascended the stairs.

A few more urgent steps and we were in the bedroom. He unwrapped his legs from around my waist and landed on the floor. The height difference pulled our lips apart.

We both stripped our shirts away and tossed them on the floor. I couldn't take my eyes off him as he shimmied out of his shoes, pants, and underwear.

The sight of his naked body did something to my insides. I walked toward him and cupped his face. The kiss I gave him was soft and gentle.

When I backed away and looked into his eyes, he knew that kiss meant something to me. This was all new to me. I needed him to be patient with me.

"You've never done this before," Jonas said.

I shook my head. "Not with a man."

Jonas smiled at me. "Not technically a man."

A shiver ran through me. Not a shiver of disgust. It was a shiver of desire. It was turning me on that he was a wolf. A wolf with the body of an angel.

"I'll let you be my Alpha," Jonas said as he undid the fly and zipper on my jeans. He sank to his knees at my feet and peeled my jeans open. His hot mouth covered my cock through my underwear. He mouthed, nibbled, and licked my length through the thin material. Satisfied, he hauled my jeans and underwear off my hips. My hard cock sprung free.

He caught my fixed gaze, held my cock, and licked a long line along the entire underside. I groaned and nearly closed my eyes. But I didn't want to take my eyes off his beautiful face.

I ran my hand into his dark hair to keep him looking up at me. He pulled one of my balls between his lips and moaned as he sucked and rotated my sac in his mouth.

He released it and moved to the other. Not a single second did he take his eyes off me. It wasn't until he moved to my cock that we broke eye contact.

His mouth was glorious, knowing the perfect suction and swirls with his tongue to drive my cock wild. Close to cumming, he pumped my length a few times and rose to his feet.

He pulled me toward the bed. I stepped out of my clothes that had pooled around my ankles, placed one knee on the bed, and lowered myself onto him. Our lips met again. This time with more urgency. Our cocks were hard between us. Jonas squirmed beneath me, and then his legs were back around my waist. He pulled me closer to him, his heels on my ass cheeks.

"Fuck me," he whispered and cupped my face. "Fill me."

My mind went a little hazy. The opportunity to fuck raw was a dream. It took a second for my brain to remind me that males of the wolf species could get pregnant.

"I'm not in heat," Jonas said, reading the uncertainty on my face.

I dove at his mouth as my cock pulsed. I'm not sure what that meant *in heat,* but Jonas seemed to think it made a difference. That was good enough for me.

I rocked my cock against his body. His hands clutched my shoulders, and he threw his head back as I attacked his throat with my lips and tongue. His body arched up and he groaned as I moved to the area between his neck and shoulder and gnawed at his flesh.

He kept whispering, "Yes, yes," beneath his breath.

This area of his skin tasted different.

I traveled from there to the soft skin behind his ear as I ground my hips against him, our cocks fighting for space. The scent there behind his earlobe was overpowering. So much musk.

My desire for him ramped up, creating a coil in my gut.

A coil that could only be quenched one way.

I lifted myself from him and encouraged him to roll onto his stomach. I peppered kisses all over the back of his neck. Jonas spread his legs and angled his ass up.

"Lube ... I don't have any," I said.

Jonas thrust his ass up higher. "We don't need any. I am *so* wet for you."

I blinked.

Wet?

I decided to believe him. I ran my finger around his hole. It *was* dripping wet. A small rivulet of fluid ran onto his balls. I guided my cock toward the opening that would change my world.

I was slow as I sank into him. Fully seated, I layered myself on Jonas' back. I intertwined my fingers with his, pulled my cock away, and thrust into him.

Jonas groaned and wiggled his ass. He wanted more from me.

My next thrust pierced him higher.

And that's when the sounds started.

With each rock of my hips, Jonas swore and shouted for *more* and *harder*. After setting a pace that bordered on violence, Jonas opened his throat and ... howled—loud and clear.

I'd never experienced anything so primal.

My cock jumped inside him. I snuffled around at the back of his neck. His scent had increased. I chased it to the area behind his ear. I inhaled deeply and opened myself to his sound.

I convulsed, jerked, and spilled everything I had left into him.

I lay still, caught my breath, and decided to roll off him. I was sufficiently bigger than him that I didn't want to impede his breathing.

Jonas hummed as he turned onto his back.

"You all right?" I asked.

He stroked his hand along my arm. "I made a mess of your bedding."

I looked over past him. He'd cum all over my comforter. I would need to invest in a washer and dryer. Jonas sat up and swung his legs off the bed. He looked like he was preparing to leave.

"Where are you going?"

"Back to work."

I stroked his back with my fingers down along his spine. "Not yet. I want to hold you."

Jonas looked over his shoulder at me. He looked surprised.

"You sure?"

I hauled on his arm. "Come back."

He crept along the bed toward me and arranged himself in my open arms; his head on my shoulder—his hand on my chest. I closed my eyes and soaked in the moment.

I'd had sex with a man, and it had been incredible.

I exhaled and tugged Jonas tighter to me.

I'd had sex with a wolf.

I turned my head and inhaled the scent of him.

"What are you doing?" Jonas asked.

"You smell incredible."

"You can smell that?"

"You? Yeah."

"That's unusual for a human. And I've rutted with a few."
Rutted?

"Not many?" I asked.

"It's frowned upon in the wolf community."

"And yet you do it anyway."

"I don't like rules."

"Don't packs insist on them."

"My brother is the pack leader. I'm permitted indiscretions."

I turned his face to me and kissed him. "I'll have to thank your brother."

Jonas giggled and tucked closer to me. "Wouldn't that be a sight?" He stroked my chest and played with the thick hair. "Lucas … thank you for letting me rut with your brother."

"Okay." I rolled a little. "Why do you say rutting?"

"It's the equivalent of your fucking. It means casual sex. And your *making love* … we say mating. That only happens between wolves who are committed to each other."

"So, we just rutted."

Jonas touched my face. "Yes, and it was *so* good."

"You howled."

"You hit all the right spots."

I rolled Jonas so I was back on top of him. I took my time kissing him. He wrapped his arms around my neck. I wanted to remember everything about him. His taste—his scent. The feel of his incredible body beneath me. He'd be haunting my dreams for some time.

Jonas stroked his hand through my hair. "I really do need to go. Dinner rush."

Against the wishes of my body, I let Jonas up. We dressed in silence, and he followed me down the stairs to the front door of the store.

Jonas rose on his toes and kissed me. He sank onto his heels. "Back to rivals."

I simply nodded. I couldn't speak. I would've begged him to stay.

Chapter Five | Jonas

I attempted my best pirouette, grinning, once I was back behind the counter of my restaurant. The dinner crowd was drifting in. Even the grumpy humans couldn't dampen my mood.

It had been an impulse, walking back across the street and knocking on the door to Damon's apartment. When I saw the desperate look on his face, I knew I had made the right decision.

The rutting had been incredible. The tender kisses—unexpected but welcome. It had been a long time since I felt cherished. He'd held me so tenderly I'd almost shed a tear.

"Any specials tonight?" one of my regulars asked me.

"I'm feeling generous. 15% off anything on the menu."

I was going to fly on this high as long as I could. Tomorrow, we'd be rivals again.

There had been additional tension between us. Now that was out of the way, we could go back to trying to undermine each other's businesses.

According to some flyers, Damon's bistro would open in 2 days.

Creekside Deli

Such a non-inventive name. People would remember it, though. The humans were bound to flock to him. We didn't have a delicatessen in Creekside. I was sure Damon had curated a selection of food items humans would be snapping up. He was right, in addition to purchasing his likely high-priced food, humans would stick around. Experience the products firsthand.

I closed my eyes and remembered his fingers locked in mine as he pounded me into the bed. A mixture of the aggression I liked with a touch of tenderness. And his kisses.

I sighed and faced the kitchen.

Heavenly.

I tied my apron around my waist. It couldn't happen again. I'd never rutted with a human more than once. My brother allowed me a level of transgressions, but even he had limits.

I couldn't tell him I had rutted with my competition. Not after he'd stuck his neck out and asked the West Creekside pack to join him in boycotting Damon's business.

I needed to tell someone, though.

Me: *"Adam?"*

Adam: *"Just a second."*

Adam was probably dealing with one of the pups. Sometimes it was hard to talk and do at the same time. Like when you were rutting. The inner conversations shut down entirely.

Adam: *"Okay. What's up?"*

Me: *"You absolutely cannot tell Lucas."*

Adam: *"Sounds yummy but I can't promise anything."*

Me: *"It doesn't impact the pack."*

Adam: *"Then spill."*

Me: *"I rutted with Damon."*

Adam: *"Your restaurant competition?"*

Me: *"Yeah, there was a weird tension between us."*

I busied myself wiping down the counters and setting out coffee cups and cutlery. There were always a few humans who liked to sit and treat the counter like a bar. I'd heard plenty of sob stories over the years. Acted like a bit of a therapist.

Adam: *"Like sexual tension?"*

Me: *"Yeah, it was intense. I went across the street, grabbed him, and kissed him at the bottom of the stairs to his apartment."*

Adam: *"Just like that?"*

Me: *"Yeah. We needed to get it out of the way so we could go back to our corners. One thing led to another, but the rutting was amazing. Angry and tender. He had me howling."*

Adam: *"Sounds romantic."*

Me: *"Stop. It was a good time, nothing else."*

Adam: *"You going to see him again?"*

Me: *"Not a chance. I never rut with the same human twice."*

Adam: *"That's right. I forgot he was human."* A short pause. *"Is it any different ... rutting with a human?"*

Me: *"Are you thinking about bringing in a human third?"*

Adam: *"Haha. No, I'm just curious."*

Me: *"They smell different."*

Adam: *"The rotting vegetation?"*

Me: *"No, that's never bothered me. Just not as much musk. And the scent of their seed is subtle. I could tell though, that Damon had spilled seed right before I kissed him."*

Adam: *"Do you think he was thinking about you when he did."*

Me: *"Guaranteed. He practically attacked me on the stairs. After the kiss, I went to leave, and he held the door closed so I couldn't. It was such a sexy power move."*

Adam: *"You couldn't resist?"*

Me: *"He's gorgeous and he's commanding. How could I?"*

Adam: *"Do you* like *him?"*

Me: *"I enjoyed him. It won't happen again."*

Adam: *"You're sure about that?"*

Me: *"Positive."*

A human slid onto a stool at the counter.

Me: *"I have to go. Customers."*

Adam: *"Have a good night."*

I handed the human a menu. "Can I get you a cup of coffee to start?"

"Can I have a beer? Domestic."

"You know we don't serve alcohol."

"A guy can hope you've changed your mind about that."

"We're a family diner. I won't be introducing a drinks menu."

"Fine. I'll have a cola. Easy on the ice."

As I was turning to fill a glass with cola, a scent caught my attention. Caught my cock's attention too. I nearly dropped the glass when Damon walked through the door into my diner.

My body vibrated, stunned. I finished pouring the cola and set it in front of the customer. Damon took a stool at the far end of the counter away from anyone.

I drifted down there to him and leaned on the counter.

"What are you doing here?"

Damon smiled at me. "I hear your burgers are good."

"They are but your kitchen must be fully stocked by now."

"My kitchen doesn't come with everything I'm craving."

My breathing stopped in my chest. Was Damon flirting with me? We'd already rutted. We were supposed to go back to being competitors. He was in enemy territory.

"Why are you here? Really."

"I told you. I'm hungry and I want to try one of your burgers."

Damon perused the menu as I stared at him. He chewed on his bottom lip as his eyes scanned the food choices. I inhaled his scent, and it made my mind buzz.

His lips looked delicious.

I remembered them on my body.

"Can I get the mushroom burger?" Damon asked oblivious to the fact memories of our rutting session had caused my cock to tent my apron.

He was human. He wouldn't be able to smell my arousal.

"Sure. Coming right up." I turned quickly toward the kitchen. Away from his sight and that of the rest of the restaurant. I concentrated hard on what was happening in the kitchen.

My cock thankfully behaved.

"Mushroom burger," I called to the kitchen. I was glad when I turned around and saw another two humans sitting at the counter. I could stay busy. Keep my mind off Damon.

I served Damon his burger without any further dialog. As he ate, my counter filled up. While dashing from one customer to the next, I managed to slip Damon his bill.

I didn't even see him leave. I went to his place and picked up the cash he had left me. He had tipped me generously. As I was tucking the merchant portion of the bill into the cash register, I caught the sight of writing at the bottom. I lifted it back out and read Damon's words.

"I'll be waiting for you."

My heart thundered in my chest as I read it again. I felt queasy in my stomach. Queasy in a desperate need kind of way. I could feel my face flush.

"Can I have some more coffee?"

My mind snapped back to the present.

"Sure. I'm on it." I retrieved the coffee pot and refilled the human's cup. I left them with two more creamers and a packet of sugar to replenish what they had used.

The rest of the night did little to distract me. Damon was on my mind. The words of his note playing on repeat. The memory of our afternoon together spread desire through me.

It was my turn to close the restaurant. After I took out the garbage, I switched off the lights. I took one last look around to make sure everything was in order and locked the door.

I turned and faced the building across the road.

The lights were on upstairs.

I couldn't do it.

It might mean something if I did. I walked around to the side of my building and climbed into my truck. The entire drive home, I imagined Damon expecting me. The thought of him sitting there waiting for me made me sad. To reject him like that had been incredibly difficult.

TWO DAYS LATER, Creekside Deli across the street opened. There was a steady stream of humans coming and going, arms laden with packages and bags.

Damon had to be pleased.

I sighed.

Not going to him the other night was constantly on my mind. It shattered me that I had probably hurt him. That he had gone to bed alone when I could have been there wrapped in his arms. Covered in his gentle kisses. That I could've fallen asleep with him.

Dammit.

I went to my office and slammed the door. I hauled a handful of tissues out of the box and dabbed at my face. It wasn't the first time imagining him waiting for me had brought me to tears.

This was killing me.

Dammit again.

I left my office and came out from behind the counter. I didn't even take off my apron. I headed out through the door and across the street like I was being pulled by a magnet.

I entered Creekside Deli. Damon was busy behind the butcher case filling a human's orders. Piling butcher paper high in cuts of beef steaks.

He was focused on what he was doing until he spotted me.

Damon excused himself, saying he'd be back in a second. He had his arms crossed, scowling, as he approached me. "What do you want?"

Damn. Not again.

Tears streaked down my cheeks. Surprise and then concern softened Damon's features. He rushed to me and placed his hands on my arms.

"Jeezus, Jonas. What's wrong?"

"I'm sorry," I managed. "I'm so sorry."

"Sorry about what?"

I exhaled and swallowed as more tears raced down my face. "I left you waiting."

Damon bit his bottom lip. "Don't be sorry. I get it. It didn't mean as much to you … what we did. I shouldn't have come to you and put you on the spot like that."

Oh, God.

I shook my head. "No. I felt it too, but I was scared."

There. I had admitted it to Damon and myself. The tenderness Damon had shown me after we rutted had formed a crack in the armor I kept around my heart.

I wanted more of that.

But he was human.

The thought of keeping this going terrified me.

Damon pulled me into a hug. The tightness of his arms— the feel of his breath on my cheek. What I felt for him was more than my cock needing a rut.

"What time are you off work?" Damon asked.

"Whenever your store closes."

"I'll make dinner."

We separated before the humans noticed we were holding each other too long. As it was, they were going to talk. A human and a wolf hugging each other in public was unheard of.

This small action would make its way back to my brother. I didn't care.

"When do you close?" I asked.

"Six but I'll have dinner ready by seven."

I almost brought up my dietary restrictions, but I knew Damon was aware. The thought of eating in front of him made me nervous, but I needed that time with him.

This was more than just rutting.

"I'll see you at seven," I said.

Damon's face spread into a smile. "I'll be waiting."

"I promise I won't run this time."

"I know."

The whole way back to the restaurant, it felt like my feet weren't touching the ground. The hours until 7 crawled by. The dinner rush over, my manager was able to finish the night.

I inhaled a long breath as I pulled open the doors to Damon's store.

He shouted down the stairs at me. "Can you lock those behind you?"

"For sure." I locked the doors and headed toward where his voice had called down to me. Up the stairs and into his kitchen. I didn't remember much about the space. We had been busy devouring each other on the way through it. And after rutting with Damon, I'd been floating on a cloud, oblivious to my surroundings. It smelled good once you filtered out the cooked food.

"Sit," Damon said. "Can I get you anything to drink? Water?"

"Do you have beer?"

Damon opened the fridge. "I didn't know you could drink beer."

"Some grains and fermented vegetables once in a while don't hurt us."

"Good to know." He set a beer in front of me then turned and busied himself at the counter. He returned to me with a plate. Two thick raw steaks were stacked on it, blood pooling beneath them. My inner wolf saw red, and the room disappeared. I remember lifting one to my mouth.

When I emerged from my feeding frenzy, Damon was sitting across from me, staring.

He hadn't touched his food.

He pointed at my mouth. "Can I see? I noticed while you were eating."

It took me a second to figure out what he was talking about. Then it clicked. My canines had descended while I was feeding. My gums ached as I forced them to descend again.

I peeled back my lips. I couldn't help but growl. It felt strange striking such a menacing pose toward someone I had no intention of harming.

Damon's eyes opened wide, and he swallowed hard.

I was surprised when he rose from his seat and approached me. Even more surprised when he cupped my face. I relaxed my mouth and accepted the kiss he lay on my bloody lips.

It was not the response I had been expecting.

"I'd like to leave the kitchen," Damon whispered to me. His voice almost sounded nervous. I inhaled the incredible scent of him. He was aroused and his cock was seeping precum.

I allowed my canines to recede.

"You haven't eaten your dinner."

"I'm no longer hungry for food. Only you."

I didn't hesitate. I scrambled to my feet and into his arms, our mouths reconnecting. I jumped up on my tiptoes to increase the pressure. He pressed his tongue into my mouth, tentatively.

He hummed as he rolled his tongue over mine.

For a second, I'd been concerned. My mouth would taste like blood. Most humans wouldn't like that. It didn't bother Damon at all. His tongue was everywhere as we deepened the kiss.

It *was* time to leave the kitchen.

Reluctantly, we pulled away from each other. Damon led me, holding my hand, through the living room and into his bedroom. As I lay on the bed, I gazed up at him. His cheeks were covered in bloody smears. I looked at my hands. I hadn't cleaned them.

He didn't care.

Damon crawled onto me and took my mouth, swirling his tongue everywhere, tasting everything. The primal urge in him surged desire through my veins.

I wanted him.

He unbuttoned and unzipped my pants and hauled them and my underwear off my hips. He was like a creature possessed. The look in his eyes was hunger.

He didn't waste a second. My cock was in his mouth before I had a chance to ask him if he was sure about it. This was only his second time with a male. I had thought he'd hesitate.

I clutched the bedding as he sucked my length and played with my cockhead. He used his tongue to lick my slit and he groaned and lapped up every bit of my precum.

Then my cock was back in his mouth. His technique wasn't perfect, but his exuberance made up for the lack of experience. He was loving having my cock ride his tongue.

Damon stopped and pulled my pants off the rest of the way. At the foot of the bed, he scrambled out of his clothes. As he did so, I dispensed with my shirt.

Finally naked, he was back on top of me the way I remembered from the last time. The pressure—the feel of his skin. The scent of him. His kiss was gentle.

I parted my legs.

I was so ready for him.

"Will it work facing you?" Damon asked. "I want to see your face."

"Of course, it will." I stroked his jawline with my fingers. "You're gorgeous."

"And you take my breath away."

I moved one leg and bumped it into his arm until he got the message and moved it. I put my leg over his shoulder, my heel resting near the base of his neck.

He was quicker to move his second arm. After I lifted my leg to his shoulder, I pulled him down for a kiss to reassure him. This time would be different.

I could feel it.

Damon guided his cock and pressed against my opening. I reminded myself to relax as he pushed into me. He adjusted his arms and sank deeper. I nearly blissed out it felt so good.

"Baby, yes," I whispered as he seated himself against my ass. He leaned forward and caressed my lips with his. We stayed like that for the longest time. Just enjoying each other.

He moved away and then thrust into me.

I didn't dare close my eyes. His gaze on mine was ravenous but warm. He cared about me. I clung to him as he rocked steadily against me. There was no harsh pounding this time.

I didn't beg him for it—he didn't instigate it.

This felt like mating.

I felt a tear escape my eye and trickle into my ear. Damon leaned toward me and kissed the tract of wetness it had left behind.

I dug my hands into his hair and pulled him toward my mouth and then held him against me; his face tucked into the space between my shoulder and neck.

He kissed my skin and licked the claiming area.

"You taste different here," he whispered to me.

"That spot is sacred. It links wolves together as mates."

"Mm."

I threw my head back, moaning and mewling as he sucked the sacred spot into his mouth and ran his teeth across it. I clung to his back, digging my fingernails in. He continued to thrust into me, so gentle—and loving. The combined feeling overwhelmed me.

"Do it," I whispered, my voice gravely and hoarse.

How he knew what I was asking him to do, I'd have to talk to him about later. Even though it wouldn't link us telepathically, it would be a clear message of our intention.

He bit down as hard as he could, barely breaking the skin.

I howled. A wailing howl of commitment.

My canines descended as Damon released me from his teeth. He pushed himself away and looked down at me. I could smell my blood on him. His thrusting stopped.

He ran his thumb across my bottom lip, then down one canine.

We didn't need to speak.

He came back to me, hovering near my face. His hips rocked his cock into me; his rhythm returned. He kissed my shoulder, exposing his neck to me.

I found where his claiming area would be if he was a wolf and dragged my teeth and tongue across it. Damon shivered and his cock pulsed inside me.

My inner wolf started screaming, *"Mate."*

My body took over and I sank my teeth into Damon's flesh. He groaned out a low scream, his hips stilling. His blood filled my mouth. I wanted to suck hard—to feel that connection with him.

To link to him.

I knew it wouldn't come.

Damon was human. If we'd said the words, I would have been mated to a human.

Fear rolled through me.

I wanted it. I wanted it *so* bad.

I was shocked when Damon's breathing deepened, and he started drilling his cock into me again. Clinging to me and thrusting; his ass clenching.

I released my biting hold on his flesh.

"That's it, baby," I whispered. "Cum for me."

A few final pushes and Damon grunted and filled me. Then collapsed in my arms. I wrapped them around him and kissed the side of his head. He tucked his hands under my shoulders and clung to me. My cock was good for now.

"What did we just do?" Damon asked.

"We came a few words short of claiming each other as mates."

Damon exhaled. "I think we might be in deep."

"Eh. You're growing on me."

Damon laughed and lifted himself away from me. He rolled off me onto his back. The bite marks looked bad. I hadn't meant to bite him that hard.

"We need to take care of those." I touched near the bite. "Do you have a first aid kit?"

"In the bathroom."

"Let's go, then."

Damon grumbled but he led the way to the bathroom. He washed his face first, and so did I, and rinsed my mouth, and then I had him sit on the toilet as I cleaned and dressed the wound. The breaks in my skin would be fine. I had a wolf's immune system.

Back in the bedroom, Damon pulled back the covers on the bed. He climbed in and waved me toward him. I couldn't have resisted if I tried. His warm arms encircled me as I joined him.

Sleep came easy. We woke and … my mind stumbled. We woke and *mated* twice more. Each time gentler and more loving than the last.

Damon was right.

We were in deep.

Chapter Six | Damon

I awoke to the sound of soft breathing. It was still early. Only a small amount of light was making its way inside my bedroom through the curtains. I rolled onto my side to look at him.

Not only did Jonas have the body of an angel … he also had the face of one.

It was difficult to reconcile that with the face he had presented me with at the kitchen table. Lips drawn back, bloody canines protruding. His eyes dark green. Or the way he snarled as he ripped into the raw meat—holding it with his bare hands, blood dripping down his chin.

He wasn't human.

And yet I yearned for him.

What was growing between us was more than just sex. I touched the wad of bandaging covering the bite marks he had given me. The pain had subsided to a dull ache.

He said we had stopped short of uttering words that would make us mates.

I wondered what those words would be.

I rested my hand between our faces. I could feel his breath on my fingers. I wanted to touch his lips. To stroke them. To wake him so we could get lost in each other again.

His lips pulled into a smile, and he opened his eyes.

"Good morning," he said.

"It certainly is. It was a good night too."

"It certainly was." Jonas smirked at me. "I'd like to do it again."

"That can be arranged." I wrapped my hand around the back of Jonas' neck and pulled him to me for a kiss. It was just as perfect as every kiss I'd shared with him.

"I'm opening the restaurant this morning." Jonas ran his fingers through the hair above my ear. "So, I have to go. But maybe we can see each other again tonight?"

"Will your pack figure out you're staying in town again?"

Jonas exhaled. I'd hit on something. "It's possible. My scent won't be at home in the morning."

"I don't want to get you in trouble."

Jonas launched himself at me, looking like a springing cat, and lay on top of me. He grabbed my face and joined our lips. I was breathless by the time he pulled away.

"I'll see you tonight. I'm off at 11." With that, Jonas climbed out of bed. I watched him dress, saddened as each part of his beautiful, responsive body was covered up.

He came back for another kiss—short and sweet this time.

Then I was alone.

And it hurt—my craving was so intense for Jonas, it frightened me.

I SWEAR, his shadow blocked my entire doorway, the wolf that entered my shop. A few of my customers for valid reasons decided they were going to leave.

They were scared. I probably should be too.

I knew who this was. Jonas had mentioned that our hugging in my store would start a rumor mill that would likely reach his brother's ears. Neither of us had expected a visit.

"You must be Lucas," I said and extended my hand to him.

He didn't take it. Crossed his arms instead.

"Is your name Damon?"

Then his gaze landed on the white bandage visible beyond my shirt collar. He rushed at me and pulled my shirt aside. His voice came out low and rumbling. "What is this?"

"I had an accident." I swallowed. "A work accident."

"I can smell him on you."

"Who?"

"Don't play stupid. My brother, Jonas has been here with you. I can smell his seed."

That shouldn't be possible. I'd had a shower. I started trembling and nausea overwhelmed me. He had come for me. Meeting the Alpha leader under these circumstances wasn't on my wish list.

My knees threatened to give out.

"Once. He was here once." Jonas had told me one transgression would be permitted. The fact we had met up twice would not sit well with his brother.

"Take that bandage off."

"What?" I gathered some unexpected courage and knocked his hand away. "No."

"Do it now, human!" I was positive the building shook under my feet. His voice had certainly rattled the windows. Windows with human faces peering inside.

Jeezus.

"Okay." I peeled at the tape. "But we didn't say any words."

That didn't appease the vicious look on Lucas' face. If anything, it made him madder. I had confirmed what he suspected. I finished removing the tape and lifted the square bandage.

He exhaled as he stared at the two puncture marks on my skin.

"How many times?" he asked. "How many times did you mate?"

"That's personal."

Lucas stepped forward and wrapped his thick hand around my throat. "Human … you are going to tell me, or I am going to tear into your jugular and end your life."

A strong and confident voice from the doorway startled me.

"Four," Jonas shouted. "We made love four times."

Lucas shoved me and I fell backward, landing on my ass. He turned to face Jonas.

"Don't you dare use human terms for what you did."

"It's what we *did*, Alpha. I was with a human who made me feel loved."

Jonas walked around Lucas and helped me up from the floor. Once I was on my feet, he wrapped his arm around my waist. It felt good to be held by him. I knew I was protected in his presence. He was a good foot shorter than me … but he made me feel protected.

I focused on the words Jonas had spoken.

I had made Jonas feel loved.

He deserved that. Jonas deserved to feel loved. We'd spent a lot of time whispering stories of our lives to each other last night in between sleeping and enjoying each other's bodies.

Jonas was precious. But I could tell there were deep scars. There were topics he avoided by changing the subject. And there was sadness. So much sadness, it broke my heart.

"We'll talk about this at home," Lucas said.

"I don't live in that house anymore," Jonas replied.

"That's not what I meant, and you know it. Adam needs to weigh in on this."

"This has nothing to do with the pack."

Oh, God.

And there he was again, looming—even angrier.

Lucas moved toward us, snarling.

"What did you say?"

"This is between Damon and me. We have things to work out. I'll keep the pack in mind but ultimately it's our decision where this goes from here."

"There are pack members *as we speak* building *your* house. And you're telling me you have no regard for what they might think about this?"

"Think about what? That I found someone I enjoy being with? Why does it matter if he's a human? What difference does it make? Why should it affect the pack?"

Lucas growled; his lips peeled back.

"Because you can't have pups with a human!" he roared. Again, the glass in the windows rattled. I gripped Jonas' hand. I hadn't known that he couldn't get pregnant by me. Jonas had only mentioned he wasn't in heat. Not that I couldn't even get him pregnant in the first place.

"Is that what I am to you?" Jonas replied. "A pup producing Omega?"

"You know that's not true." Lucas frowned. "I know you desperately long for pups. You'll never have them if you become mates with this human."

I turned to Jonas. Maybe that's where some of the sadness came from. His desire for *pups*. I didn't want to hold him back from that. Anything we had wasn't headed in that direction.

"Jonas," I said. "Maybe we should end this."

"What? No. We've made a connection."

I pulled away from him. "Maybe you felt something. I'm not sure anymore."

"But you bit me. You practically claimed me."

"I was caught up in the moment." I backed away further. This was going to hurt—both of us. I didn't want to bring Jonas any more sadness, but it needed to be done.

"It meant nothing," I added.

Jonas stared at me then took off running. My front door slammed behind him. I could see him tearing across the street and down the side of his building. Seconds later, his truck backed out onto the street, screeched its tires, and sped away. I was left with Lucas.

"Stay away from him," he warned.

"That's the plan."

Lucas grunted at me, then turned and left.

When he was gone, I collapsed onto my knees, put my hands over my face, and wept.

THREE WEEKS PASSED, and I was still in pain. I longed for him. I went to bed each night and cried myself to sleep. He'd done something to me—deep inside.

I peered through the front window of my shop. If I stood at the exact right angle, I could sometimes catch glimpses of Jonas working behind the counter of his restaurant.

I had spent far too much time standing there over the weeks we'd been apart. We'd only met up twice, but he had come to mean so much to me. Like my compass had finally found North.

Customers were waiting. I needed to pitch in and help. I'd hired two employees. They worked in the front of the store, selling deli meats and fresh-cut beef, pork, bison, and chicken.

My place was in the kitchen. All 6 tables and 3 booths were happily eating. I'd adjusted my menu, so I wasn't competing directly with Jonas. My menu included charcuterie boards, plowman's lunches, gourmet salads, and fancy desserts. All things he didn't offer.

I stepped behind the butcher case. "What can I get you?"

"2 of those seasoned ribeyes and 4 Cajun spiced chicken breasts, please.

"Do you want all 4 chicken breasts wrapped together?"

"No, sorry. 2 and 2."

I ripped a sheet of butcher paper off the roll and went to work choosing and wrapping the cuts of meat for the customer. I was operating on muscle memory. My mind was elsewhere.

Jonas, of course.

And a hunting trip I had planned for tomorrow. I'd suggested to my regular customers that I was thinking of adding wild game and they were all for it.

I was hoping to bag a deer. Maybe some rabbits. I could get rabbits from my meat supplier but those were raised caged. They didn't taste the same as wild.

I'd invested in two new pieces of equipment. A smoker and a sausage maker. My customers had been particularly interested in venison links.

Raw venison sausages were something I would have prepared for Jonas when he eventually stayed for breakfast. My gut churned. I had loved waking up with him.

I could still picture his sleeping face.

"Can I get you anything else?" I handed the packages to the customer.

"Could I try 2 of those zucchini boats?"

"Sure. I'll write the cooking instructions on the package."

"Perfect. Thank you."

Back to ripping and wrapping. I peered at the restaurant area. People were finishing up. I'd need to bring bills and clear tables. I thanked the customer after handing her the last package.

The tips were generous at all the tables. I brought the bin out from the back and started loading dirty dishes and cutlery into it. That was the end of the lunch rush.

I turned away from the tables and spotted a figure in the street outside my store. It was Jonas and he was staring at me through the window. When he saw I had seen him, he went back into his restaurant. It wasn't the first time he'd done that. It was a weekly occurrence, but those were only the times I caught him. My heart wanted me to run out into the street, wrap him up in my arms, and tell him I was sorry and that my feelings had grown for him as well.

But I couldn't do that to him.

I couldn't make him truly happy. He wanted a family. A mate and pups. I had no way of giving him that. He deserved those things. It might be the only thing that could lift his sadness.

I sighed and went into the kitchen. I wore many hats back there. I was the only one in the back. Preparing food and washing dishes were both my jobs.

The hot water felt good. I concentrated on what I was doing, trying my best to be mindful. It was a technique that sometimes worked.

I stopped and closed my eyes. The feel of Jonas' lips on mine filled my mind.

I whimpered and went back to washing. A tear ran down my cheek.

I was never going to get over him.

I closed the store late. We still had customers filing in until 8 pm. I sent my employees home and managed the store on my own. The restaurant portion was closed. I was able to handle everything alone. By the time I switched off the light and went upstairs, I was exhausted.

My sleep was fitful. Not sure why I had trouble sleeping other than my brain was always working overtime. The night Jonas slept over; my mind had been peaceful.

He had calmed me like no one else ever had.

I was tired the next morning. Not tired enough to call off my plans. But tired enough that I brought an entire thermos of black coffee with me.

It was an hour's drive to Riverton. Another fifteen minutes trying to find the pack leader's house without GPS. I drove up the long gravel driveway and approached the front door.

Now that I'd experienced Lucas, I felt prepared to speak to this leader, Mark.

Pretty sure it was Mark who opened the door. He practically filled the opening. He invited me inside. I hadn't expected that. I had planned on paying cash at the door, completing our contract.

"Sit," Mark said.

I did as I was told. My body felt like it didn't have any other choice. I had no intention of making this Alpha male angry. Whatever he asked—I would do.

"What are you planning on hunting?"

"I just need one deer."

"You're a good shot? I don't want any animals suffering."

"I kill on the first shot."

"I expect you to dress the animal on site. Leave the entrails for wolves."

"I can do that."

Mark crossed his arms. Towering over me. He hadn't taken a seat.

"What's happening between you and Jonas Black?"

Why on earth was this relevant?

"Nothing. We met up twice, then I ended things."

"I don't want you approaching any of my wolves."

That's why it was relevant. He didn't want a lowly human *coming on* to his wolves. Maybe lead one of them astray. I had no intention of ever *rutting* with a wolf again.

"That's not a problem. It was a one-time experiment."

Mark snorted. "You dishonored him."

"I didn't mean to. I had no idea meeting up with him would cause so much trouble."

"Did you apologize to Lucas?"

Was I supposed to?

"No, I didn't know I needed to do that."

"You *do* need to do that."

"Okay, I will." That was going to be difficult being so close to where Jonas lived. He'd told me the cabin he lived in was 20 minutes east of the main house.

"Is this going to affect my permission to hunt on your territory?" I asked.

"Not this time. I expect you'll have apologized before your next hunting trip, though."

I needed some important information. Jonas was right. Humans had no access to wolf territory maps. The librarian had practically laughed at me.

"How far until I hit Creekside territory?"

Mark scowled. "A human walking. Not sure. It takes us three hours at a good pace in wolf form." That's all I needed to know. If I didn't walk any longer than three hours east, I was safe.

"Thank you." I dug around in the pocket of my hunting vest and pulled out the wad of cash that would cover the cost of permission to hunt the Riverton pack's territory. I planned to hunt once a week. It was costing me $200 a trip. Paid a month in advance.

The wild game better sell. Profits were slim as it was.

I handed him the $800.

"Our business is concluded," Mark said. I took that to mean I could stand again. I rose and followed Mark back to the front door. He peered out at my 4x4 truck.

"Follow our driveway into the forest. It goes quite a way in. You won't have any trouble with *that* vehicle. Parts of the road get a bit rough."

"Perfect." I extended my hand. Mark's grip was tighter than Adam's had been. Mark's rough handshake was a message. Don't fuck with him.

The road was flat for about 2 minutes. After that, it became narrow, branches hitting the side of my truck. And it was bumpy as all hell. Mark hadn't been lying.

After 10 minutes, the road ran out. Trees rose into an incredible canopy in front of me. It only took me a minute to collect my gear. I started my trek into the woods. Due east.

After thirty minutes, I started looking for animal trails. There was a lake very close to my location. Deer would head down there to drink.

I saw what looked to be an animal trail ahead of me. I backed up slowly and found a fallen log to hide behind. The slight breeze was in my favor. I waited.

After about an hour, a young buck walked into view. His rack was still growing. I aimed my rifle and took the shot. He dropped to the ground—dead.

I'd kept my promise of one shot.

The bushes rustled to my right. I fell back and re-aimed my rifle as a black wolf stepped out from the underbrush. It wasn't a big wolf and it seemed content to just look at me.

A member of the Riverton pack. I lowered my rifle. I wasn't in any danger. Mark had probably sent the wolf to spy on me. Make sure I wasn't committing any offenses.

The wolf wandered closer to me, head down, crept right up to me, and nudged my hand. She wanted me to pet her. I assumed she was a female because of her smaller size.

I ran my fingers through the fur on top of her head and gave her a rub. She moved closer and pressed her body against me. I stroked the thick fur on her back a few times.

She whined when I stopped and nudged my chin. It was an intense experience being this close to a wild animal. I used both hands to smooth the fur of her face, muzzle to ears.

Her eyes gazed into mine. Emerald green. Her soul radiated from those eyes. They reminded me of Jonas. A howl sounded behind me. She whined again and turned and ran off.

I was in a daze as I dressed the deer. Methodical, I soon had it wrapped in its hide. I left the entrails spread all over the ground. Maybe the black wolf would come back and have a feast.

I had a feeling she was long gone, though.

It was an experience I wouldn't forget anytime soon.

It took me longer to pack out to my truck than it did to trek in, the heavy weight of the deer on my back. Finally, at my truck, I tossed the deer into my truck bed.

The road felt bumpier on the way back out. Probably because I was tired. Being in the forest had refreshed me while I'd been in it. The wolf had pumped up my adrenaline, making the gutting and cutting quicker. Now, back in my truck, I wanted to go to bed.

The deer went straight into the small walk-in fridge in the store's kitchen. I unwrapped it and hung it on a meat hook. I'd cut it up after I had a couple of hours of sleep.

I was fast asleep when a sorrowful sound startled me awake. It was the saddest sound I'd ever heard. It was a lone wolf howling. It sounded like it was in pain.

Jonas.

It had to be. I curled up and covered my ears. The sound was tearing my heart apart. Tears gathered in my eyes. What had I done to him to make him sing a song like that?

I pictured the black wolf's eyes I had gazed into today.

The tears spilled down my face and I screamed to drown out the sound.

Jonas.

The wolf I had encountered in the forest today.

It had been my Jonas.

Chapter Seven | Jonas

I wandered back into the forest just outside town. I hadn't been able to stop myself. I'd seen Damon load his rifle into his truck. I knew where he was going. I'd driven into Riverton, parked my truck, and headed into the woods. He was easy to find, his scent was imprinted in my mind.

Approaching him had been stupid. I had only meant to watch him. Be close to him. But my desire to be near him had pulled my body to him. I needed him to touch me.

His hands had felt so good. On my head. Down my back. A different sensation than when we were entwined in bed, him touching, teasing, and tasting every inch of my skin.

The Riverside pack had detected me. I had managed to get back to my truck and drive off before they caught up with me. There would be a report made to Lucas about one of his wolves traipsing around in Riverton territory. Any admonishment would not negate the feeling of joy I had experienced as Damon stroked me. My heart had broken all over again when I left him.

It hit me when I was in the alley behind the restaurant. I shifted to wolf form and sang a song of regret and anguish. It had spilled from me, reliving every heartache I'd ever had.

The peak of the song came from that part in my heart that Damon had stolen.

I trotted toward home. I needed the comfort of those four walls. I also needed to run there in wolf form. Tire myself out so I wouldn't end up in bed crying myself to sleep again.

I reached the cabin, shifted, and let myself in. I headed straight for the bed. I'd spread bear furs out on it. They brought me comfort. Reminded me of cuddling up to my carrier when I was a young pup. I didn't have many memories of that time in my life—but that one had remained.

I curled up on the furs.

It meant nothing.

Those words of Damon's haunted me. I touched the spot where he had bitten me. If he'd known the ceremonial words, Damon would have spoken them.

I knew that deep in my soul.

It had felt like destiny. From the first time I kissed him, I knew he was my Alpha. A chosen mate I could have spent my entire life with.

I would've given up a life with pups for him, but he had chosen to abandon me instead. Maybe I was wrong. Maybe he spoke the truth. That he'd been caught up in the moment and bitten me.

I'm not sure what me sadder. That he had feelings for me and pushed me away. Or that he had never had feelings for me in the first place.

I decided to hunt. Back in wolf form, my mind shifted. Survival thoughts dominated much of my consciousness. My inner wolf might allow me some peace.

I took off into the darkness of the trees. This was my third shift of the day. I might be in incredible discomfort when I shifted back, my bones popping in and out of shape.

I found a warren of rabbits beneath a tree stump. I dug around until one of the rabbits got scared enough to bolt. I chased it down and grabbed it by the throat. Gave it a good shake to kill it. I wanted to head back. Something was pulling me to be there.

As I jogged back, a scent filled my nostrils.

The pull.

I stopped outside the cabin door.

Sitting with his back against it—Damon.

"I know it was you," Damon said. "I could tell by your eyes."

I dropped the rabbit on the ground.

"Can you understand me when you're like this?" Damon asked.

I barked once. I hoped that would answer his question.

"Okay, good. Because I have things I need to say to you."

I sat to listen. My wolf brain was getting in the way. I had to listen carefully.

"Here's the truth. It *did* mean something to me when I bit you. I wasn't simply caught up in the moment. There was a surge of desire to make you mine, I wanted you so badly."

Damon had understood what he was doing—and he'd done it with intent. I looked down at my rabbit. It was calling to me. I set my gaze back on Damon. My inner wolf could wait.

I'd make sure of it.

The shift started. I kept my attention on Damon. He would either sit through it or he would take off in a panic. There were very few humans who had seen a wolf shift. Some I'd rutted with had asked me to shift for them. I'd only obliged a human once and then things had gotten weird.

That wasn't a kink I was into.

Damon reached behind him and gripped the door frame, a look that was a mix of horror and curiosity scattered across his face. His eyes were wide—his mouth open.

I finished the shift.

The emotion of everything he'd said hit me like a charging maternal moose. My inner wolf had been protecting my heart. I stayed on my knees.

"Baby … why? Why would you do that to me? Discard me like that."

"I did it for you. You want pups. I can't give them to you."

"So you decided for me? What I want in life?"

"I thought it was for the best."

"Well, you thought wrong. I would gladly give up having pups to be with you."

"You would?"

I scrambled to my feet and went to him. I kneeled in front of him and took his hands. "I don't think you get it fully." I paused. In the past, bringing this up had ended several relationships. No one ever wanted me once my mind and body longed for them this desperately.

Damon touched my face, his fingers stroking my cheek.

"You can tell me anything."

I sought comfort in his gaze. His eyes exuded such adoration that it made it easier to speak. I placed my forehead on his. "I think I might be falling in love with you."

Damon lifted my chin and kissed me and lingered. It was a reassuring kiss. One of longing and commitment. He wasn't going to walk away from me.

Our lips separated.

I didn't expect him to say it back.

"How did you find me?" I asked.

"I don't know. I parked on the road at the bottom of the driveway and started walking. Your scent filled my mind. When it left my mind, I changed direction until it filled me again."

"Oh, baby—." I grabbed Damon's face and kissed him. My heart sang in my chest. Every molecule of my body vibrated. I was flying. I released his mouth and gazed into his eyes.

"What?" Damon asked. "Was that weird? It was weird, wasn't it?"

"No, baby … it was glorious." I brushed my thumbs across his cheeks, still holding Damon's face. "It means somewhere in your ancestry; you had a wolf."

"There was a wolf in my family?"

"Yes, maybe even more than one."

"That's why I could sense you?"

"Yes … baby, you *are* my Alpha."

"What does that mean?"

"It means that if you were fully wolf, you would be my fated mate."

"Is that why we were drawn to each other?"

"It would have been impossible to fight it."

Damon came at me for another kiss. This one was more desperate. He wrapped his arms around me, pulling me off balance. I fell against him. Our lips parted.

We ended up in a hug.

"Does that mean I might be able to give you pups?" Damon whispered in my ear.

My stomach did a little flip and it felt like someone was standing on my chest. I gripped him tighter. He was perfect. My mate—he was perfection.

"It's possible," I said.

Damon put his hands on my shoulders and separated us. His gaze looked very serious. My Alpha licked his lips, uncertain. "Is that something we want to try for?"

It felt like my heart dropped into my stomach.

"You want … you want pups … with me?"

"I want everything with you. You've become the one bright light in my life."

Such a surge of emotion swept up my body. My inner Omega was breaking down in tears. I never imagined I'd ever be having this conversation. There was only one answer.

I'd gone into heat this morning. There was no better time to try.

"Then, yes. Yes, we *do* want to try."

Damon rose to his feet, bringing me with him. He reached back, opened the cabin door, and led me inside. He held me in his arms as he kissed me. The commitment was on his lips again. I'd found the one. The one meant for me. The one who would make me feel whole.

The one to lift my intense sadness.

I sat on the bed as he undressed. I lay back and welcomed him into my arms. The pressure of his body on mine made me feel safe. Damon was my Alpha.

My fated mate.

I hummed and wrapped my legs around Damon's waist, our mouths exploring; my mind processing what we had agreed to. My mate found his way to what I knew was one of his favorite places; the soft skin behind my ear where my scent gland was.

He licked and inhaled, quenching his need to be filled by my scent. He moved to my collarbone and kissed from one shoulder to the other. Down my sternum. Over from one nipple to the other, sucking hard until they were hard sensitive nubs.

He pinched one between his thumb and forefinger as he brushed his lips back and forth across my belly. He lay a gentle kiss at its center. I brushed my hand through his hair. I knew why he was there, spending so much time. I could practically hear his prayer that my belly be filled with life.

I was no longer falling.

I loved him.

Tears ran down both cheeks into my hair. I closed my eyes and moaned as Damon sucked my cock into his mouth. Even his mouth was gentle. The suction was firm and loving.

He ran his tongue around my cockhead, and sucked the cap. My cock was leaking heavily for him. I'd never wanted anyone so desperately. I was going to lose control.

He was all I needed.

I was never going to be the same.

He was in my veins.

My mate.

Damon shuffled down the bed and lifted my legs. I took them in my hands, hanging on behind my knees. His curious tongue licked the area between my balls and my hole. I could feel his hot breath where I needed him to be. His hands were on my ass cheeks, holding me open.

I whimpered as his tongue dove at my hole. My Omega hole that was his alone now. Damon prodded at the tight muscle, his tongue piercing and licking. I relaxed to allow him in.

I could feel my wetness run in a stream down to my lower back. Damon chased it with his mouth, sucking up every drop he could find. He capped my hole with his tongue to catch the flow seeping from it. Giving his tongue a rest, he slid a finger into my hole.

I groaned as he added a second finger and ran them across my sensitive gland. He reached further. My body clamped down on his fingers as he found my cervix.

He withdrew his fingers and held my gaze as he sucked on them.

Fuck.

"Baby, I need you." I let go of my legs and reached for him. "Alpha, please."

Damon crawled up, causing the bed to shift back and forth, and covered my mouth with his lips, kissing me. I moaned as I sought out every taste of myself in his mouth.

I cupped his face and held his gaze as he guided his cock to my hole. I bit my bottom lip. His cock passed my relaxed ring in one steady thrust.

"Fill me with your seed," I whispered as I stroked his cheeks. "Put a pup in me."

Tears filled his eyes, ran down his nose, and dripped on my face. One landed on my lip. I licked it away, every salty bit of it.

"Anything for you," he replied. "Absolutely anything." He thrust his hips, gliding in and out of me. He started to increase his pace. Every part of me lit up. I felt a rush from the heat that had overtaken me when I awoke without him this morning. Another reason I had followed him.

My body was aching for him.

"My Alpha." I watched his eyes as he increased his pace.

"My Omega."

I smiled. He'd used a wolf term for me. *My Omega*. He understood what this meant to me. This time it would be different. It really would mean something.

"I want to be yours," I said, starting the ceremony.

He looked puzzled.

"I want to be yours," I said again. It took Damon a second to figure out where I was going with my words. Then realization and understanding sparked in his eyes.

He kept rocking me into the furs.

"I want to be yours," Damon responded.

"You have to be first," I prompted and turned my head to expose the claiming area between my shoulder and neck. Damon wrapped his arms around my body, kept pumping his hips—and bit into me. This time, he broke the skin completely.

I howled, letting the message reach the rest of the pack. I was claimed by my Alpha. My fated mate. I rolled Damon until he was on his back. My canines descended.

This time, Damon simulated my howl as I sunk my teeth into him and sucked. My mind buzzed with the taste of him. But no telepathic connection. No sharing of thoughts.

But he was still my Alpha. I had claimed him.

An invisible force had pulled us together.

Blood dripping down my chin, I joined his song.

The pack heard me. Some joined in. Some didn't. Adam's voice was loud and clear. Lucas' voice was absent. It crushed me that my brother wasn't overjoyed for me.

Damon flipped me over onto my back; his pace interrupted only by our song. He raised one of my legs and caressed his cock into me, sweeping back and forth over that sweet spot.

"Baby," I whispered, and came all over my stomach.

Damon leaned forward and whispered a kiss across my lips.

"My beautiful Omega."

"Fill me, Alpha." I tightened my hole around him, the full length of his cock. It was what he needed. Damon grunted and spilled his precious seed inside me.

After a few more slow strokes, he collapsed beside me and laughed softly.

"What's so funny?" I asked.

"I'm married to a wolf."

"That you are." I smiled. "Hey, what's your last name? I want to take it."

Damon turned his head to look at me. "Lister."

I ran it through my head first. "Jonas Lister. I like the sound of that."

"You're so precious to me." Damon held my chin and brushed his thumb along my bottom lip. "I love you, Jonas. My sweet Omega."

There it was. The three words I'd longed for all my life.

Those same words formed easily on my lips.

"I love you too."

Chapter Eight | Damon

We hadn't left the cozy cabin for three days. That's all the time either of us could spare. Our employees had to run things while we were gone. Jonas was only in heat for a few days twice a year. It was possible to become pregnant at other times, but it wasn't typical.

In between sleep and words of love, I'd filled him with so much of my *seed* that he couldn't walk across the room without it running down the inside of his thighs.

We were hopeful that one of those seeds had gotten through. That one of those seeds was compatible with Jonas' egg. Sometime this week, we would know.

I tugged Jonas into my arms. We were in my apartment. He had stayed overnight—again. My mate had stayed in my bed. A bed I didn't want him to leave.

Jonas mumbled something in his sleep then sat up.

He had a wild expression on his face.

"What is it?" I rubbed his back.

"Fuck!" Jonas clapped his hand over his mouth, leaped off the bed, and ran out the bedroom door. The reason for his urgency was answered when the sound of vomiting came from the bathroom. I couldn't contain the ridiculous grin on my face as I raced to his side.

I stroked his hair and caressed his shoulders with each violent upheaval. In between throwing up, Jonas was laughing. He was giddy. This was the answer we'd been waiting for.

We were going to be parents.

I kissed the back of his head. "I think you need to move in with me. We should be living together now that we're married and expecting a pup."

Jonas nodded his head in agreement as he clung to the toilet seat. He slid onto his ass beside the tub. "I'll have to clear it with Lucas first."

"How is that going to go?"

"I'll be honest. Not good. I doubt I'll get my brother's permission."

"Then why bother?"

"It's protocol. I'm willing to go against the pack in some ways, but I'd like to try to stick to as many of the rules as possible. It won't stop me from moving in with you, though."

I exhaled. There was so much that was foreign to me. Pack life sounded complicated. I needed to catch up. Jonas wouldn't be joining my human world. I'd be joining his wolf one.

"Should we both go?" I asked.

"That would be expected."

Jonas rolled toward the toilet again and dry heaved into it.

I rubbed his neck. "What can I do to help?"

"Fresh ginger. And lots of it. I can make tea with it. It should help."

"Should I go now? The grocery store should be open."

"Please. I'll be fine here with my new porcelain friend."

He lifted his head, and I kissed his cheek. "Okay, my sweet Omega. I'll be right back." I dressed, retrieved my wallet, and headed out the door. My shop didn't open for another hour. I had plenty of time to buy ginger and make Jonas some tea to quell his nausea.

Thankfully, the grocery store *was* open. I cleared out the entire ginger section. While walking home, I had a strange sensation come over me. The jerk and tug were unexpected.

I found myself in an alley alongside one of the houses on the main street. Two ominous men loomed over me. I dropped the bag of ginger. Not men—wolves.

A fist found my face before I had a chance to protect myself. Not that trying to avoid the subsequent pummeling would have made any difference. As I lay on the ground alone in pain and bleeding, I thanked whatever gods that might exist for sparing me from death.

Those two wolves could have easily killed me.

They'd only been ordered to deter me.

Lucas.

He wanted me to leave town. To leave his brother and run back to where I had come from. He underestimated me. I wouldn't be threatened into leaving my family.

Because that's what Jonas and my unborn pup were.

They were my family.

I rolled onto my side. The ginger was scattered all over the ground, crushed into the gravel. A few people gathered at the end of the alley. One guy ran to me and squatted down.

"Someone has gone for help," he said.

I looked at him and realized only one of my eyes was open enough to see him. My face and my stomach had taken the brunt of the beating. And my ribs. It felt like some were broken.

I groaned as an ambulance pulled up and two emergency workers jumped out and pulled a stretcher out of the back. Surely, I wasn't that bad. I was proven wrong when they tried to have me stand and lay on the stretcher myself. I felt it now. The wolves had broken both of my legs.

In the ambulance, I grabbed onto the ambulance attendant riding with me.

"I need to get a message to my husband."

"Sure. Do you have a number for him?"

The only place I had a phone was in the shop. If Jonas was still hanging over the toilet, he might not answer it. He might not answer it anyway. It was my business phone.

"There's no phone. Can the sheriff stop by? It's the apartment above Creekside Deli." I closed the one eye I still could and exhaled. The front door of the shop was locked.

Would Jonas answer the door if he heard someone pounding on it?

I drifted for a moment. As soon as I was in the ambulance, they had started an IV drip that I suspected contained pain medication. It was making my thinking hazy.

The store would open soon. One of my employees had a key. I felt better. By the time the sheriff got there, the front door would be unlocked.

A warbly voice washed in.

"We'll give the sheriff a call. Don't worry. Your husband will be informed."

"Thank you."

I shuddered out a sigh. I was close to tears. How could Lucas do this to his brother? Jonas and I loved each other. We were fated mates. We had a pup on the way.

I was human ... that's how.

I let the pain medication take me. The pain resurfaced when I was manhandled for radiographs and CT scans. I started crying when the doctor said I needed surgery.

I needed my Jonas with me.

I was scared and I needed him.

One last agonizing transfer and I was on the operating table. That's the last thing I remembered until I opened my one eye in a different room. A young woman approached my bedside.

"You're okay, Mr. Lister. You're out of surgery. This is the recovery room."

"Damon," I croaked.

"We'll need to keep you here a while longer, Damon, but your husband is waiting to see you."

Oh, thank God.

I couldn't help but nod off, an image of Jonas' face in my mind. When I awoke, the image was still there. I blinked and smiled. It *was* him sitting at my bedside, holding my hand.

In the corner of the room, another figure caught my eye.

Lucas.

My heart thundered and I gripped Jonas' hand far too tightly.

"It's all right," Jonas whispered to me. "He's here to make sure you're all right. Two of the wolves went rogue and attacked you. What happened to you had nothing to do with Lucas."

With this new information, I only had one thought on my mind.

"Why didn't they kill me?"

Lucas stepped toward the bed. "Out of respect for me. Jonas is my brother."

"What's going to happen to them?"

"I expelled them from the pack. One of them was our sister's mate." Lucas looked distraught. That had to have been hard for him. "Adam was in agreement ... as was our sister."

Jonas reached across the bedrail and stroked my face. "I told Lucas about the pup." He smiled at me. "He suspected when I kept running to the restroom in the waiting room."

I looked at Lucas, trying to gauge his reaction.

"Congratulations." Lucas' response was terse, but I also detected sincerity. He had to be happy for Jonas. His brother had found his fated mate and was starting a family with him.

I lifted my hand to touch Jonas' fingers on my face.

A tear trickled down my cheek.

"My beautiful Omega."

Lucas cleared his throat. "I'll be going. I'll let the pack know you're on the mend."

I pried my gaze off Jonas' face to look at Lucas.

"Thank you," I said to him.

"You're part of the pack now, Alpha," Lucas said. "We'll pick up the pace to finish the home for you and your family. It'll be done by the time Jonas whelps the pup."

I grinned as Lucas left the room. The door swung closed.

"He called me Alpha."

Jonas rose to his feet, hung over the bedrail, and kissed my forehead.

"We had a long talk. I told him how you found the cabin. And then, of course, there's the pup. He agrees, there was a wolf in your ancestry. He believes you're my fated mate."

"And this house you're having built?"

Jonas sighed. "I know you asked me to move into your apartment with you, but it would make more sense for us to have a house with space to run around and lots of extra bedrooms."

"You planning to fill them?"

Jonas grinned at me. "Maybe?"

"You Blacks are going to take over the entire pack."

"I'm not a Black anymore."

I closed my one good eye. I was exhausted.

"That's true. You're my mate now."

"My Alpha … sleep." Jonas kissed the bridge of my nose.

BY THE TIME they released me from the hospital, Jonas was showing. He looked adorable. All happy and in full-on nesting mode. The house had been finished as promised. There was a bit of post-construction cleanup to do, but Jonas had already had the nursery painted pale yellow.

He was gnawing at bones to pick out furnishings for it.

I wasn't going to be much use. Having two broken legs meant my mobility was limited. One was worse than the other. At least, the stronger one could support my weight if I used crutches.

We bumped along the long driveway with Jonas driving. This would be my first time seeing the house that would be our home. Jonas took the truck over a bit of the clearing. The driveway didn't go all the way to our house yet. That was the next project. I felt bad not being able to help.

The pack had come through for us. I was stunned when Jonas told me we owned the house outright. The money to pay for the build had been contributed by the other members.

Jonas said it would be partially furnished. Every family from the pack would contribute to help furnish our home. I smiled and held Jonas' hand as we pulled up outside our house.

I felt loved. While I was in the hospital, there hadn't been a single day when a member of the pack hadn't shown up to sit with me. Adam especially. He told me he had a special place in his heart for Jonas. And then he'd told me why. I hadn't been able to stop laughing.

I could imagine Jonas putting on the charm and trying to pick up Adam.

I looked out through the truck window at our home.

Grey siding and white shutters in Craftsman style with a big porch out front. I could imagine us sitting out there watching our pups running around.

Pups and grandpups.

Jonas came around to my side of the truck and opened the door. Two wolves who had sat with me on occasion in the hospital, Lance and William, raced to my side and helped me from the truck.

I shrieked, then laughed as William lifted me into his bulky arms and carried me up the stairs to the front door. He deposited me outside it and handed me a key.

"Don't really need a key," he said. "No one would dare break in."

"It's customary," Jonas said. "For the Alpha to unlock the door to their new home."

I took the key. This was monumental. Unlocking a home for my family to live in. I never thought I'd ever have a family to love. My love life to date had been disastrous.

I was here with Jonas now. I inserted the key and turned the lock. It clicked and I swung the door open. I was stunned. The interior was beautiful. Dried husk-colored walls, white trim, and gorgeous hardwood floors. To the right was an office, and then the space opened up. Massive kitchen with dark cabinets and marble countertops adjoining an eating area and family room.

To one side, a set of stairs. Jonas had arranged the office as a bedroom for us until my casts were off and I could use stairs again. I'd have to wait to see the nursery.

Jonas led me over to the solitary piece of furniture in the family room. A sofa that looked cozy enough to sleep on. It had been a long day already. After leaving the hospital, I checked in on the store. The new chef was doing well cooking and managing the whole business. I'd been lucky to find him. If it hadn't been for Lucas calling in a favor, I might have been in trouble.

I never in my life imagined I'd have a wolf managing my business. He'd even taken over the upstairs apartment. I had visions of him trying to fit on that queen-sized bed.

Perhaps he'd replaced it.

It seemed my customers had adjusted to a wolf running the place. The store was full. Even the restaurant side of things had more patrons than I would have expected.

I stretched out on the sofa.

"Would you be more comfortable in bed?" Jonas asked.

"No, I'm fine here. I don't want to be away from where you are."

"I'll just be fussing around in the kitchen. I have boxes of dishes and things to put away." He smiled at me. "Human stuff. I might even learn how to cook."

I laughed. "I'll look forward to seeing that."

"Which reminds me." Jonas went to the fridge and pulled it open. "I brought some sandwiches from the restaurant. Do you want one?"

"No. I just need sleep."

I closed my eyes and hummed with contentment as Jonas lay a blanket on me. I pulled it up around my neck. For summer, it was cool. Probably because we were in the shade of tall trees.

I dozed for a few hours. I awoke to the smell of bacon and eggs cooking. Jonas was moving back and forth in the kitchen, dashing between the stove and a toaster.

"You need any help?"

Jonas waved me away. "No, I've got this. I've seen it done enough times."

He looked a little comical. I could tell he was getting flustered. Timing was important when it came to fried eggs. He seemed to be managing, though.

He slid the whole frying pan full of food onto a plate. He had overestimated the amount of food I could consume. I was happy to try my best. I was starving.

I sat up and swiveled, placing my feet on the floor, so Jonas could put the plate on my lap. He handed me a fork and knife. I gazed across what he had cooked for me. The bacon looked perfect. Even the eggs looked like they'd retained some runniness. I smiled.

He'd even put jam on my toast.

"I've always wondered about that." Jonas pointed at the bacon.

"Do you want to try some? It's just meat."

"It smells really good when it's cooking."

"That is the consensus of 99% of the population of the world."

Jonas lifted a piece and smelled it. "Does it taste like boar?"

"Not quite. Boar is sweeter and nuttier."

"Hm." Jonas nibbled the end of the piece he was holding. Then took a decent bite. He furrowed his brow. "What is that taste? It pinches my tongue."

"Salt. Bacon is cured with salt."

"Huh." Jonas took another bite and chewed happily on it. "I like it."

"Do you want to try the eggs?"

"Yuck, no. Cooked eggs? I have my limits."

"Thank you for making this."

"I'm serious. I'm going to master this cooking thing."

"You do remember, I'm a chef, right?" I teased.

"Doesn't mean I can't pitch in when you're too tired to cook."

"I appreciate that."

I set to work eating the mountain of food Jonas had cooked for me. He hadn't been too far off. I ate my way through most of it, including the orange juice he scurried into the room. He'd been paying attention to what was happening in his restaurant kitchen over the years.

Everything was excellent.

Now I needed to try out our new bed.

With Jonas' help, I hobbled into the office turned bedroom, and to the bed's edge. It took both of us to swing my legs onto the bed. Once I was there, Jonas climbed onto the bed with me.

He tucked himself into the crook of my neck and clung to my chest. I pulled him as tight as I could to me and kissed his head. It was different being in our own bed. Jonas had climbed onto my hospital bed numerous times, but there had been an element of satisfaction missing.

"Why don't you shuffle down a little," I said.

Jonas raised his head and looked at me. "Really?"

"I've missed you … and your body."

"Mm, yum." Jonas grinned at me, then crept down my body, being mindful of my casts. I lifted my ass a little as he pulled my sweatpants and underwear off my hips.

My cock was already swelling for him.

He straddled my shins, leaned forward, and sucked my cock into his mouth. I arched my back and moaned. The relief was overwhelming. I had been dreaming about him.

Thrusting into and filling him.

My cock hit the back of his throat. He coughed around my girth but kept going. Slurping and sucking. Jacking me in his fist. He sucked on my cap, then climbed off the bed.

He made quick work of shedding his clothes.

When he climbed back on, he straddled my thighs. He reached back and guided my hard cock inside his perfect body. I held him around his waist as he seated himself on me.

I brushed my thumbs back and forth over the outer edge of his swelling belly.

Jonas rose and fell on me, then kicked his head back. He'd been craving this as much as I had. The last time we'd made love, we hadn't known we were pregnant.

This time felt different.

We were building a life together. An incredible life.

Jonas groaned as he rode me. He leaned back and put his hands on my thighs. The change in position sent his cock bouncing. I wrapped my hand around it and stroked him. He was leaking precum so profusely it was gathering on the fingers of my closed fist.

I used it to coat his cock, reducing the friction.

Jonas switched from groaning to mewling softly, pumping his cock into my hand. Leaving one hand on my thigh, he brought the other to one of his nipples and pinched it.

A small bead of white appeared at its tip. He ran his finger over the liquid and looked down at me. He placed his finger in my mouth. The subtle taste … my cock pulsed.

My beautiful Omega was already lactating. His body was primed for the birth of our pup. It might have been the light, but a halo appeared to form above his head.

I chose to believe it was a halo.

He truly was an angel.

My angel.

Jonas leaned forward and kissed me. His thrusting slowed as he explored my mouth. Then he was back, seated and rocking my cock in and out of his body.

He lowered a hand to his cock and strangled it hard. It wasn't enough to stop the flood of his seed that spattered over my stomach and chest.

I clung to his hips, setting his pace.

He whined and cried my name as pressure built in my cock. I yelled loud enough to alert the other houses around us as I spilled into the love of my life.

Jonas let my body slow, then cupped my face, and kissed me.

He was reluctant, but my cock had softened and slipped from him. He was soon back in my arms, nuzzling the side of my neck. I wrapped him in the blanket we had knocked aside.

"When did the milk start?" I turned Jonas' head and kissed his forehead.

"Yesterday. Caught me by surprise. I was thinking about the pup."

"Only three more weeks."

"Yeah." Jonas lowered his hand to his belly. I didn't like how quiet he was. He usually sounded more excited about the pup. Jonas sighed and kissed the side of my neck.

"What's wrong?"

"I'm afraid it's going to be a runt like me."

"First off, you're not a runt. You fit perfectly with my body." I stroked his hair. "You couldn't be more perfect. What's going on that has you worried?"

Jonas rubbed his belly. "Three weeks out, I should be bigger than this."

"Compared to whom? Adam? Have you seen the size of him?"

"Something seems wrong."

"Sweet Omega." I shuffled out from under his head enough that I could look down on him. "What do you want to do? We can do anything you want?"

Jonas frowned. "I want to get one of those human scans. Like when Adam had the twins."

"Then that's what we'll do." I hated the look of concern on his face. "Okay?"

Jonas nodded. "Thank you."

I laid back down. "Everything will be fine."

Chapter Nine | Jonas

It felt like we had waited forever already. The hospital was busy. The waiting room we were in was filled with pregnant human females. They kept glancing at me. It was obvious that Damon and I were a couple. I had a firm grip on his hand.

It wouldn't take too much calculation on the humans' part to figure out I was the one who was pregnant. I was barely showing but I had a habit of resting my hand on my belly and rubbing little circles on it like the pup could feel me. Maybe they could.

"Jonas Lister?"

I took a deep breath and joined Damon as he rose to his feet with the help of his crutches. We were led down a long corridor and into a darkened room.

I hopped up on the bed covered in crunchy paper. Damon set his crutches to one side and took a chair at the end of the bed but kept a hand around my ankle to soothe me.

"Okay." The technician shook a bottle. "Lift your shirt and lower the top of your pants a little and we'll see what we've got." After I did, some warm liquid was squirted onto my skin.

I tried to relax. I kept looking at the screen, but it didn't mean anything to me. Just a bunch of white and dark patches. She swept the scanner back and forth across my belly.

"How many weeks are you?" the technician asked.

"Five."

"Hm. I haven't done a lot of these, but we shouldn't be seeing what I'm looking at."

"What does that mean?" Damon asked, almost standing.

"No need to panic. There's a heartbeat." She flicked a switch, and we could hear the thrumming sound of our pup's heart. She moved the scanner a few more times, punching keys occasionally. She was taking too long. I was starting to sweat with worry.

"Then what's wrong?" I asked.

"Well …." She stopped scanning and turned to face me. "You're right on track if you were 12 weeks pregnant. Skull and spine, arms, legs, strong heart … everything is good."

"That doesn't make any sense," Damon said. "He's only been pregnant for 5 weeks."

My heart felt as though it might leap from my chest. I was terrified. Something was wrong with our pup. I'd been correct. My body hadn't felt right. Damon leaned over and held my hand.

"I should only have 3 weeks left … what do you mean the pup looks 12 weeks?"

"I'm saying, you're on track for a 12-week-old fetus. I know you weren't expecting this but what you're having appears to be a human baby."

I thought Damon might slide onto the floor. His face had gone white. I had too many questions to panic. "What does that mean? What's going to happen to our pup? What do we do?"

The technician lay her hand on mine. "Do you mind waiting a while longer? The doctor is going to want to talk to you. He'll hopefully be able to answer all your questions."

"Hopefully?" Damon's voice was thin and high.

"This is an unusual situation." She rose to her feet and handed me a towel. "Clean off and then go back and get comfortable in the waiting room."

I patted Damon's hand. The technician wouldn't have any answers for us. We'd have to wait. That's the thing with human hospitals, there was a lot of waiting.

Right now, though … I was glad of the technology.

We took a couple of seats back amongst more pregnant human females and waited. I tried to keep my mind from racing through scenarios. None of them were good.

I inhaled and exhaled a deep breath.

"It's going to be all right," Damon said.

"I'm trying to convince myself of that."

Damon kept checking the latest of the many watches he owned. Hours passed. The waiting room emptied. We were on our own. I was worried they had forgotten about us.

"Jonas?"

Finally.

I clung to Damon's sleeve as he hobbled along, and we were led to an office. We took seats on the opposite side of the desk from the doctor. He was a young male. Human.

"Okay," he started as he tented his fingers on his desk. His brow furrowed. "I've looked at the ultrasound images and what I see there is definitely a human baby."

"But I can't have a human baby," I cried. Every emotion I'd been holding spilled out. My hands started shaking. Tears poised themselves to fall. I knew the logistics. My uterus wasn't designed to carry something as big as a human baby. It shouldn't even have been possible to become pregnant. It was the reason male humans couldn't get male Omegas pregnant.

Damon stared at me, then at the doctor. "Someone, please tell me what is going on."

"Jonas is right. His body isn't designed to carry a human baby."

Damon nearly lifted out of his seat. He gripped my hand tighter instead. "And?"

"And we don't have many options."

My entire body went numb. This wasn't happening. I placed my hand on my belly. Our pup was in there. The result of our love for one another. A miracle.

"I'd recommend you terminate," the doctor said.

Too much. I sobbed as fat tears streamed down my cheeks. I lowered my head. I wanted to disappear. I didn't want this to be happening to us. Damon reached his arm around me and hugged me. He kept kissing my head. It wasn't helping.

"What else can we try?" Damon asked with his lips still against my hair.

"Anything else would be risky," the doctor answered.

I lifted my head. "I'm willing to try risky."

"Jonas." Damon's voice was soft.

"Damon." I looked up at him. "This is our pup. We can't give up on them. Please."

Damon nodded then turned to the doctor. "We're willing to try risky."

"Okay." The doctor turned his computer screen to face us. "Here's the problem." He pointed at the screen. I leaned forward against the desk. "You have the spine and the skull here." He dragged his fingers up along a line of white spots … then I saw it.

Our pup's head.

From there, the whole picture made sense. I could make out two legs and two arms with tiny little fingers. Human fingers. And no tail.

"The fetus looks to be about 12 weeks old."

"Even though it's only been 5 weeks," Damon said.

"Wolf pups grow faster than human babies," the doctor said. "That could account for the acceleration. So, there's no telling how long the gestation period is going to be. What I do know is that Jonas' uterus can only hold about 4 pounds of baby. And that's a stretch."

"Then what do we do?" Damon asked. I was glad he was asking the questions. My mind was fixated on our pup on the screen. It was a short video. I could watch its little heartbeat.

I would do anything to keep that heartbeat going.

"We'll have to keep doing ultrasounds," the doctor replied. "Weekly. Then every couple of days. When it looks like Jonas' body can't take anymore, we'll do a cesarean section."

I heard that.

"You're going to cut me open."

"Even at 4 pounds, you can't birth a baby that big anally."

Gone were my dreams of whelping our pup in our bed. Damon with me like Lucas was for all his and Adam's whelps. Mates who never left each other's sides while their pups were born.

Damon knew what I was thinking.

"I'll be with you the whole way." He looked at the doctor. "I can be there for the surgery?"

"No. The baby will be premature. We'll need the room to be clear."

I leaned my head against Damon's shoulder. "It's all right. Everything will be all right."

"Are you sure about this?" Damon asked.

I stared at him. "How can you not be?"

"Because I love you, Omega."

"And we both love this *baby*."

"I don't want to lose you."

"I'm not going anywhere. You and me and the baby … we'll be a family. You'll see."

Damon exhaled a long breath. "Okay."

I placed my hand on the desk. "Who do we contact to set up our ultrasound appointments?"

I THOUGHT THE WEEKLY ultrasound appointments would become routine. They never were. Each week our baby grew faster than the doctor had been expecting.

Within 8 weeks, I was close to what my body could handle. I ached everywhere. The baby looked to be almost 4 pounds. Last week, the doctor put me on total bed rest. I was losing my mind. I needed more time. I wanted to make sure our home was ready for our baby.

Damon, now that one of his casts was off, had become my arms and legs, assembling the crib, and decorating the baby's room. Sometimes, I cheated and waddled to the room to sit in the rocking chair and imagine nursing the baby there. My nipples always tingled and leaked.

Today, I was behaving and relaxing in bed. I was surprised when Adam walked through my bedroom door, arms weighed down by packages and bags. We'd moved our sleeping arrangements into an actual bedroom upstairs. It was one of my favorite places in the house.

"What have you been up to?" I smiled at him. "Shopping spree?"

"I found the cutest human baby store in Riverton."

I sat up in bed. That's where I'd ordered the crib from. I'd never been there myself. I lifted my hand to take what Adam had pulled out of one of the bags.

It was a tiny yellow one-piece outfit. It had a picture of a duck on the front. It was adorable. Adam handed me another item. Another one-piece. And another—and another.

"Did you buy out the store?"

Adam raised his hand. "Wait." He retrieved a brightly colored circle with a handle attached. I'd seen human babies with them in the restaurant. They were noisy.

"Human babies like these," he said. "It's a rattle."

I laughed. "I know what it is."

Adam pouted at me. "I didn't." He gave the rattle a little shake, then put it back in one of the bags. "I picked up some fuzzy blankets and a dangly thing that hangs over the crib."

I reached for Adam's hands. He smiled and took mine.

"Thank you," I said.

"I'm excited to welcome this baby into our family. It's not what we were all expecting but Lucas and I couldn't be happier for you and Damon."

I looked down at our joined hands. "I'm scared."

Scared didn't cover it. I was terrified. The doctor had explained about the epidural block they would be using to numb me up for the surgery. It sounded horrific. If things went wrong, they would need to *knock me out*. I needed to talk to an anesthesia tech. It wasn't often wolves permitted themselves to be put under anesthesia. There wasn't a lot of data about safe and effective dosages.

"Oh, Jonas." Adam squeezed my hands. "I'm choosing to believe everything will be all right. You're a strong Omega and you have a loving mate who will be waiting for you and your baby."

I nodded.

"Damon has trouble sleeping. Always has but it's worse now. He says it's because he's scared of losing me. That he never wants to be in a world without me in it."

"He loves you very much."

"I know. I'm looking forward to the day our whole family can come home."

"How long will they keep the baby?"

"I don't know. Not long, I hope."

A voice rang out from downstairs. A voice that made me feel warm and cozy inside.

"I'm home," Damon called.

"I'm behaving," I answered. "I'm in bed."

Damon appeared in the doorway and laughed. "What happened in here? It looks like a baby store threw up on our bed?"

"I may have overdone it a little," Adam said. "Stress therapy."

"He picked out some really cute outfits," I said and held one up. This one had a cheeky looking whale on it spurting a drop of water out of its blow hole.

"Our baby will have to rotate through three outfits a day," Damon replied.

"Actually, I've been reading up on that." I lifted a book I'd been reading about human babies and what to expect. "After feeding, human babies tend to sometimes spit up the milk all over themselves and whoever happens to be holding them."

"Yes," Damon said. "I've experienced that with friends' babies."

Adam sat up straight. "You've held a human baby before?"

Damon smiled. "Briefly. Not an expert by any stretch."

"You know more than either of us two," I replied.

Damon sat on the end of the bed. "You'll be a natural, my beautiful Omega."

Adam smiled and rose from the bed. He approached the head, leaned over, and kissed me on the cheek. "I'll leave you to your lovely mate."

I gripped his arm. "Thank you for all the baby stuff. We appreciate it."

Adam winked at me. "Love you. Keep me in the loop."

"Always. Love you too." I sighed as Adam left the room. During the past 8 weeks since we received the news we were having a human baby, Adam had spared so much of his time to comfort and support me. Our friendship had become stronger.

He truly felt like a brother.

Damon surprised me from my thoughts by descending on my mouth with the urgency of someone who was in love and terrified for their lover at the same time.

I held his face and encouraged him to continue. He'd gone back to work. I missed not seeing him all day, every day. Every moment we spent together needed to be precious.

I hummed against his lips. Right now, this moment was about distracting me.

Damon moved closer and inhaled the scent behind my ear. He had told me my scent had changed slightly. Not as musky. He attributed it to the possibility of the baby being a female. We'd decided we didn't want to know the sex of the baby ahead of time.

I leaned forward and lifted my ass as Damon removed the loose dress I'd started wearing. It was stretchy and comfortable. I laid back against my wall of stacked pillows.

Damon smirked and winked at me. He was adorable. I ran my hand through his hair as he layered kisses all over my swollen belly. It was a bit of a chore, but I slid down slightly in bed until my cock was accessible. Damon angled himself under my belly and pulled my soft cock into his mouth. I tipped my back against the headboard and groaned. His mouth felt so good.

He soon had my cock hard. He caressed my balls as he sucked and bobbed. The feel of a coil twisting in my gut descended to my cock. I grunted and filled my mate's throat.

He was grinning when he lifted his head.

I looked down at my chest. Streams of milk were escaping from my nipples. Damon left my cock and hovered over the milky mess. He licked my skin beneath one nipple, cleaning it—then the other. Then he sucked one of my nipples into his mouth. The feeling of the pull was incredible.

I rotated my hips up, tipped my head back, and mewled.

Damon hummed as he suckled, cupping the small amount of swollen chest tissue in his hand. Only partially satisfied, he moved to the other, giving it the same loving treatment.

Next was my mouth. Our tongues danced as I tasted him and everything he had drawn from my body. We lingered there for the longest time, slow and gentle, reconnecting.

Damon pulled away. "I love you."

I stroked his face. "I love you too."

"What can I do for you?"

"My back is killing me."

Damon slid off the bed and I rolled onto my side after placing a few strategic pillows to support myself. I groaned as Damon's hand, covered in massage oil, caressed my lower spine and the muscles on both flanks. It was a daily routine.

"Ultrasound tomorrow," Damon said.

"I think it might be time this time." The pain in my lower back was becoming incredible. And there was an unsettling dragging feeling on my rectum area. In addition to Damon massaging me, I spent a lot of time in the big tub in our ensuite bathroom. The hot water was soothing.

I lay my hand on my belly. In this position, the baby always started to stir, thumping around inside me. Not true kicks but the movement was reassuring. Our baby was alive and well.

"Did the baby wake up?" Damon asked.

"Yeah, they're jumping around in there."

Damon reached over from behind me, kissed my shoulder, and put his hand beside mine to see if he could feel the baby move. "Do you want me to rub your belly as well?"

I groaned. "Oh, that would be glorious."

Damon rearranged my pillows to support me at a comfortable incline, and I slowly rolled onto my back. He oiled up his hands and caressed the taut skin of my stomach.

I laid back to enjoy.

And fell asleep.

Chapter Ten | Damon

It felt like I had paced back and forth in the waiting room a million times. My armpit was getting sore from my crutch. I had kissed Jonas goodbye almost 3 hours ago. The staff assured me everything was all right. That Jonas hadn't been taken into surgery right away.

I don't know why they were waiting. The ultrasound showed that the baby was dangerously descended, and that Jonas' uterus was straining. His pain level had increased overnight, and he'd awoken to blood beneath him on the sheets. I had taken him to the emergency room.

An internal exam found that his cervix had started to dilate.

The baby wanted out.

Finally, someone came through the doors looking for me. "Damon?"

"Yes." I raced as best as I could over to them.

"My name is Shannon. I'm an RN here. I'm going to take you to the NICU."

"Our baby is all right?"

Shannon smiled at me. "You have a little girl. 4 pounds 2 ounces. She's tiny and delicate but she's a fighter. It must be the wolf in her."

"And Jonas is okay?"

"He's resting comfortably. You can see him in a little while."

Relief washed through me. The two beings I loved more than my own life were alive and well. And I was being taken to meet my daughter.

We approached the door to a room with windows all along the front. The lights were dim inside. "Wash your hands, then I'll need you to gown up. Gloves and mask too."

I leaned my crutch against the wall so I could follow the instructions. Once I was ready, Shannon led me into the room behind the glass. She directed me to an incubator at the far end.

I was slow to approach. I didn't know what to expect. I'd only ever seen full-term babies. My daughter was going to look different. My love for her surged me forward.

I placed my hand on the hard surface of the incubator. Inside was the most precious little person I'd ever laid eyes on. She was asleep wearing only a diaper and tubes and wires were coming off her everywhere. The nurse, Shannon, placed her hand on my arm.

"Don't be alarmed by all the stuff on her. It's there to monitor things like her temperature, heart rate, and breathing. We may need to add a feeding tube. We'll know more once Jonas is awake. We'll see if she can get sufficient nutrition from him."

"So, he'll be able to chest feed? That's important to him."

"We can try. We'll do what's best for your baby."

"How long will she be here?"

"I'm going to guess maybe 2 weeks."

I nodded my head. Jonas was going to be devastated. We'd known our baby was going to be in the hospital for a while, but now I knew how long. Those 2 weeks would drag by. The only saving grace is that we could come and see her anytime we wanted so Jonas could nurse her.

"Can I hold her?"

"Sure. Go have a seat in that rocking chair over there and I'll unhook her."

I used my crutch to get to the seat and lowered myself into it. I started sweating, I was so nervous. Shannon approached with a wrapped bundle and handed her to me.

I carefully tucked our daughter into the crook of my arm and moved the blanket away from her face. She was perfection. As she slept, she kept smacking her lips and I could feel her little fists ball up beneath the blanket. Then she stretched her legs. I bent down and kissed her forehead through my mask. That made her squirm and start to whimper. I cooed at her until she quietened.

I had spent so much time speaking to her through Jonas' belly that I felt certain she recognized my voice. That maybe it had soothed her. I hummed a song to her as she slept in my arms.

"We should put her back now," Shannon said as she returned to my side.

I reluctantly handed her back.

"Do you have a name for her yet?" she asked.

"We've talked about it. We have a few ideas. I'll need to see what Jonas says."

"Sometimes when the baby starts feeding, the … I'm sorry, I don't know what to call Jonas."

"In wolf language, he's the carrier. I don't like that. It seems impersonal. We discussed it for a long time and he's going to be Papa and I'll be Dad."

"Okay, then sometimes when the baby starts feeding, the Papa will have a rush of emotion, and the right name will come to them."

I nodded. Ultimately, it would be up to Jonas to name the baby.

"Can I see him now?"

"Let me put your daughter back. I'll make a phone call and find out."

I rocked in the chair as I waited. Once the nurse finished hooking our daughter up again, she lifted a phone on the wall near me.

I couldn't listen. All I wanted to hear was that I could see him.

She hung up the phone.

"Okay, Jonas is out of recovery. He's being moved to a room. This floor. Room 312. You can wait for him there. He'll be up in a few minutes."

I lifted my crutch off the floor and hoisted myself out of the rocking chair. I was quick to find my way down the corridor to room 312. I couldn't sit. My Jonas would be there soon.

I stayed back out of the way as two porters wheeled a gurney into the room. Jonas looked peaceful. Asleep. They transferred him into the bed far rougher than I would have liked.

Jonas opened his eyes as the porters left the room.

I clung to the bedrail as I looked down at him. I could tell by gazing into his eyes that things were a bit hazy for him. Even so, he was quick to smile when he saw me.

"Hey, gorgeous," he whispered, his voice hoarse.

I reached for his hand and clung to it. "Hey, Papa."

Jonas licked his lips. "They told me we have a female baby."

"You mean a daughter."

Jonas released a gentle laugh. "Right. Daughter." He tried to move but groaned and held his stomach. "Ouch." He looked at the IV pole beside him. "I hope that has good stuff in it."

"I think there's a button here you can push to release more pain medication."

"Push it, please."

Jonas closed his eyes. "They told me I can see our daughter in a few hours once I've rested. If I'm able to walk down to the NICU. I might even be able to try to feed her."

"I can't wait for you to see her. She's absolutely beautiful."

Jonas opened his eyes. "You've seen her?"

"Seen her and held her."

"Oh … I want that. Right now, I need to sleep, though."

I made an awkward move for the chair and hauled it to Jonas' bedside. I planted myself in it and held his hand. There was no more talking. He needed to rest so he could meet our daughter.

GOING UP THE STEPS to our home was surreal. I had been right. The two weeks until our daughter was released from the hospital had crawled by. We were at the hospital every day. If Jonas wasn't there to nurse her, he was pumping milk to give her while he wasn't there.

The only other thing breaking up the wait was my final cast being cut from my leg. It felt good being able to carry our daughter in through the front door of our home. Jonas still wasn't allowed to lift anything bigger than our daughter even though he felt like he could.

Wolves healed differently than humans. He was probably fine to do a lot of the things the doctor was restricting him from doing. The most frustrating—no mating.

I wanted to make love to my amazing perfect Omega. We'd been relegated to giving each other blowjobs. I longed to fill him with my seed again.

Without the risk of pregnancy.

A decision had been made by both of us. We weren't going to risk having any more babies. Jonas had started birth control and during his heat, we'd be using a condom.

He had wept for days after that decision.

We entered the front hall. I set the baby carrier down and smiled. Across the opening to the kitchen, a huge banner was strung from one side to the other.

Welcome Home Baby Jane!

We had decided to name our daughter after Jonas' carrier. He had fond memories of her. Jonas and his brothers had lost her when Jonas was young. Cancer in three mammary glands.

Jonas looked at me and grinned. He hadn't known our Jane would have a welcoming party waiting for her to arrive home. Adam had planned the celebration. His two oldest, Maddox and Brianna, ran up to catch a look at Jane. She was still so tiny. Her accelerated growth had stopped once she was away from Jonas' uterus. The doctor was expecting her to grow at the same rate as every other premature human baby. Maddox barked at his sister to be careful.

An Alpha leader in the making.

Adam was next to leave the kitchen and approach us. I was busy lifting Jane from the baby carrier. I didn't bother asking. I knew what Adam wanted. I handed Jane to him.

He wrapped her up in his arms and bounced her, rocking side to side. Even young wolf pups enjoyed time in the arms of their parents. Adam was a professional.

"I need to sit down," Jonas said. He was still tired all the time. The doctor said it was normal after what his body had gone through. He needed time—lots of it.

He wandered in the direction of the family room sofa.

"I forgot my wallet in the car," I said to Adam.

"No worries. I have her." Adam touched his nose to Jane's. "We have it down, don't we, sweet baby girl." He looked at me. "Yup. She says we have it covered."

I laughed. It had taken a while to get used to seeing Adam like that. In the human world, he looked like a guy who spent every day in the gym working out.

Gorgeous and muscular.

That was Adam.

The maternal nurturer that emerged around pups had seemed strange at first. Now, I admired him for it. He and Lucas were great around their pups. Loving and attentive parents both.

I headed back out to the truck.

And stopped dead at the bottom of the stairs.

Standing near the hood of my truck, a guy the size of Lucas. With black hair and dark eyes. His facial structure—he was definitely related to Lucas and Jonas.

I swallowed hard.

An Alpha wolf of incredible stature.

I refused to show any fear. "Can I help you?"

"I heard Jonas had a human baby."

I crossed my arms. "And you are?"

"His brother."

Jeezus.

It was Bryant. I'd heard everything about him and what he had done. How he had teamed up with a West Creekside pack leader and kidnapped Adam.

How Adam had almost been killed.

"You're not welcome here."

Bryant surged at me, snarling. "That's not for you to decide, human."

"This is my home. So, it *is* for me to decide."

"You live here … with Jonas?" Bryant furrowed his brow. It made him look even more vicious. If it wasn't for the fact I was used to Lucas, I'd be running right now.

"Jonas is my mate."

Bryant stepped back, almost falling. "Why did he become mates with a human?"

I didn't feel like I owed him an explanation. Jonas and I had fielded enough questions from wolves and humans alike since we claimed each other.

What was one more wolf.

"I have wolf blood in my ancestry. Jonas and I are fated mates."

"I don't believe that. Jonas used to rut with humans. You're just another rut."

What part of this is my house did he miss?

"We've claimed each other. We've taken vows. We're fated for life. Maybe you don't believe it, but Jonas and I are in love. He and our daughter are the most important beings to me."

Bryant snorted. "You're not even wolf enough to create a pup."

This wasn't going anywhere. One thing I knew—I wasn't going to let Bryant into our home. Although, I wasn't sure how I was going to stop him if he insisted.

He backed away.

"Tell Lucas I'm staying at the cabin for a few days. I'd like to talk to him."

"I'm sure he has things to say to you as well."

"Stay out of it, human. You aren't part of this pack."

I couldn't believe what came out of my mouth. Too much time around wolves?

I growled at him.

A heavy hand landed on my shoulder. "Stand down, Alpha."

Lucas stepped around me and approached Bryant. "Damon *is* part of our pack. He's Jonas' Alpha fated mate. It's not up for debate. We've all accepted him."

"I'm disappointed in you, brother," Bryant said.

Lucas laughed. "You're disappointed in *me*? That's rich." He inhaled long and hard. "Who is the Alpha male with you? I don't recognize his scent."

"I met him on the tundra. We've been hunting together."

"That's not what I asked you."

Bryant surged at Lucas snarling. I decided it was time to leave. I had no intention of watching two wolves go at it with each other. I suspected it would be terrifying.

Inside the house, I found Jonas sitting on the sofa nursing our daughter. He had his shirt off. Jane was latched to his left nipple. The other was puffy and leaking. I was amazed at how much milk Jonas' body was able to produce. He'd been pumping as well, filling the freezer so I could feed Jane in the middle of the night when I tended to be awake anyway.

I'd considered sleeping in one of the other rooms, but I couldn't bear the thought of being away from Jonas as he slept. We still had spare rooms. The two wolves who would be moving from Carina's house to ours were waiting until Jane was at least 3 months old.

Jonas' sister Carina was pregnant again. Only one pup this time. She was relieved to only be having one. After her fated mate had been forced out of the pack by Lucas for attacking me, she found another Alpha to become her chosen mate. They were still getting to know each other.

Their house was almost as crowded as Lucas and Adam's.

And he was the wolf I needed to find—Adam. I found him in the office, looking out the window at his mate and his mate's brother. They were still talking.

I put my hand on Adam's lower back. "Are you all right?"

"What's he doing back here?"

"He heard Jonas had a human baby."

"We've had 8 pups since he left. Why didn't he come back to see Lucas?"

"Maybe he feels protective over Jonas. Maybe because he had a baby instead of a pup."

"I suppose, but I don't want him here."

"I don't blame you. What he did was unforgivable."

"And yet, Lucas has forgiven him."

"I'm not sure why, except Bryant *did* release you."

Adam turned and looked at me. "Not until I was beaten and dragged through the forest by my legs. Hauled roughly enough one of my ankles broke. The pack leader planned to hang and gut me. Our sweet Maddox would have been cut out of me and killed."

Fuck.

What Adam endured had been horrific. Why *had* Lucas forgiven Bryant?

"He's staying in the cabin," I said. "Sounds like an Alpha male is with him."

"Yes, I picked up his scent. He must be staying just out of sight."

"Bryant said he met him on the tundra. That they hunt together."

"Lone wolves don't usually team up like that."

"Do you think there's more to their relationship?"

Adam wrinkled his nose. "I don't detect any of the other wolf's seed on Bryant."

"So ... just friends."

"Seems to be."

Adam left the window and headed for the front entry as Lucas walked in through the front door. I followed him. I was curious as to what had been said. They hadn't fought each other.

"Bryant is staying in the cabin with a friend," Lucas said to Adam.

"Yes, Damon filled me in on that much."

"He wants to rejoin the pack."

Adam crossed his arms. He looked close to crying.

"Bryant had no intention of letting Derek hurt you," Lucas said. "He only went along with the kidnapping because Derek promised him you would become his mate."

"Under goddamned duress."

"I believe he would have treated you well."

"I would have been his prisoner."

Lucas sighed. "He hadn't thought it through."

"I'll say. He let an Alpha male mate with him."

"He has nightmares about that."

"Good," Adam replied.

"And absolute night terrors about what happened to you."

Adam exhaled. "I should hope so."

"He's incredibly remorseful."

"Doesn't matter. It'll be up to the pack whether they let him back in."

Lucas grunted and zoned out. Adam joined him.

There was silence for a few seconds.

"What the fuck!" Jonas yelled from the family room. "Lucas, seriously?"

They must be taking a vote among the pack members.

Jane started crying.

That was my cue. I was the expert rocker and walker. Jonas had scared her by yelling. Full of milk, she needed to be burped anyway. Jonas handed her to me and joined his brother and Adam in the front entry. They were there longer than I expected.

"Fuck!" Adam screamed. Jonas flew back into the family room and threw himself onto the sofa. I kissed Jane's head. I guess they'd decided to let Bryant back in the pack. Lucas had overlooked that I wasn't in on the conversation. That I hadn't voted. I would have voted *no*.

I'd speak to him about it. Tell him, I would greatly appreciate it if they could have important meetings in person—or wolf, so I could contribute as a member of the pack.

Not being telepathically linked bothered me. Especially Jonas and me. Being able to speak to him no matter where I was would be a dream. To tell him I loved him all day—every day.

I could do that right now. He was upset.

I sat on the sofa beside him. "They voted him back in."

"Yes."

"I take it you voted *no*."

Jonas glared at me. That would be a *yes*.

"Adam is pissed. Thankfully, Lucas was smart enough to vote *no* too. The last thing Lucas and Adam need is a rift between them. Lucas isn't stupid. He did it out of respect for Adam."

"So, Lucas doesn't have any kind of veto?"

"The pack is a collective. Lucas is the leader, but he doesn't have ultimate power."

"Good to know."

Jonas closed his eyes. "I'm exhausted. Do you mind if I shift? I sleep better in wolf form. Not so much stress and worry rattling around in my head."

"No, go ahead."

Jonas had never done this before. The last time I'd seen him in wolf form was outside the cabin before we claimed each other and created our daughter.

"Thanks, baby." Jonas rolled off the sofa and landed hands and knees on the area carpet. It was more horrific watching him shift in this direction. Watching his beautiful features distort and stretch and fur grow all over his body. It took less than 30 seconds.

He lay on the carpet on his side and closed his eyes.

He was asleep before I had a chance to say, "I love you."

Even in wolf form, he was my perfect angel.

My forever love.

Chapter Eleven | Jonas

I nearly banged my head repeatedly on the hard surface of our mahogany dining room table. Adam was right, if this went on, I was going to lose my mind.

"For all that is holy," Adam said. "If you apologize one more time, Bryant, I am going to vomit all over this table."

"I need you to understand," Bryant said. "You don't have to forgive me, but you need to understand, I never would have let anyone hurt you. I knew Lucas' pack was close. I would have teamed up with them and saved you. I regretted it the moment we kidnapped you."

"I don't understand how you thought I would go with you in the first place. You saw me crawling up the steps of the house toward Lucas. He's my fated mate. Done deal."

Bryant shook his head. "I wasn't thinking. I just knew I wanted you."

Lucas had called a family meeting. We were holding it outside of our telepathic link so Damon could be included. It felt weird sitting across from each other at our table.

Bryant's return to the pack was the subject of discussion.

"If I accept your apology, will you please drop it?" Adam asked. "I get it. You had no ill intent toward me. I just don't understand why you were willing to go to such extremes. Mating and being claimed by an Alpha male. That had to have been degrading."

Bryant looked at the table. "I would have done anything to be with you."

"Did I feel like a fated mate to you?"

Bryant lifted his face and set his gaze on Adam. "That's what it felt like. The pull."

Adam turned to Lucas. "Have you ever heard about anything like that before?"

"A one-sided fated mate attraction? It's rare but it can happen. Our sire's brother had the same thing happen to him. Maybe there's some hereditary component to it."

Adam sighed. "Okay, Bryant. I forgive you. You had little control over what you were doing."

Bryant groaned as he let out a long breath. "Thank you, Adam."

"Do you still have those feelings?" our sister Carina asked.

Bryant furrowed his brow. "No, they disappeared when I hit the tundra. Even being across the table from Adam ... I feel nothing other than affinity because Adam is Lucas' fated mate."

"So, we won't have any more problems?" I asked.

"None," Bryant replied.

"What about this friend of yours," Carina said. "We don't know anything about him."

"He's harmless. He was part of a pack that disappeared. Lack of pups."

"I've heard of that happening a lot more recently," I said. Stories of packs not being able to keep their numbers up were becoming more common. Even West Creekside was having a problem. I suspected it was one of the reasons the old leader, Derek, had kidnapped Adam and planned to kill him. He didn't want Lucas to gain an advantage by having a strong fated Omega mate.

"We just hunt together," Bryant said.

"You're not too crowded in that cabin?" Adam asked.

"We'll make it work. I'm used to him. I've known him for years."

"Is he planning to join the pack?" Damon asked.

Bryant shook his head. "Not likely. He likes his solitude."

"*Your* link with our pack isn't giving you any problems?" Lucas asked.

"I can still hear whisperings from the West Creekside pack, but it's disappearing. Drowned out by *our* pack's chatter. I think it helps that Derek is long gone."

Lucas nodded. He looked around the table at everyone. "Does anyone still have issues with Bryant being part of the pack again?"

Every single one of us shook our heads *no*. Bryant had apologized sufficiently and explained why he'd done it. The call of a fated mate was impossible to ignore. He'd simply reacted.

Stupidly. But that was our Bryant.

We all rose from our seats and headed outside.

Lucas, Bryant, Carina, and I would hunt together now.

Shifted to wolf form, we approached Bryant and gathered around him. It felt good to rub against him and touch our noses. Lucas started the song of joy. We all joined in.

Our family was complete again.

IT WASN'T USUAL but we had brought Jane to bed with us. It was nap time for her, and we wanted to lie on either side of her and watch her sleep. She truly was a miracle.

We were able to kiss each other over the top of her sleeping form.

"I love you," Damon whispered to me.

I fell back against his lips and held his face in one hand. I brushed my fingers through his hair. Damon was everything

I had ever wanted in a mate. All the sadness and self-loathing I'd carried with me for years had melted away. The universe had brought my fated mate to me.

He was my Alpha.

I would be with him until the end of time.

Did you love this story? Do you want to read about Bryant and his love story?

Look for ***Alphas' Omega*** by JT Fader
An MMM Wolf Shifter MPreg Romance

About the Author

JT Fader is an alternate pen name for Leigh Jarrett (she/he), allowing Leigh to explore their love of MM+ paranormal and fantasy stories by creating their own worlds.

In their hometown of Victoria, BC, Canada, Leigh can be found nestled up with their fabulously supportive wife and trusty laptop or enjoying the wondrous Vancouver Island outdoors.

To stay up to date with JT Fader's new releases and promos, check out their JT Fader Fantasticals website at www.jtfader.com.

You can also find Leigh on Bluesky.